Boys, Broken

Boys, Broken

A Novel

Jonathan Mitchell

Copyright © 2019 Jonathan Mitchell
All rights reserved
ISBN – 13: 978-1-0950-1-4103

To Nick, who told me to keep going.
And to Lauren, for telling me when to stop.

Prologue

It was spring, and they were running, he remembers. Running for their lives. At least, that's how the dream always seemed to start. Every single night, Matthew Rode has this dream. It is the same one he has had since he was a teenager, and if asked, which he almost always was, would insist it really happened the way he saw it when his eyes were closed, his breathing slow and steady, the world at night unaware of what terrible visions rest inside.

Twenty years, damn.

Every few nights or so, as the trazadone begins to take hold and he feels the world begin to slip away, he has the same cold vision.

They were just a couple of stupid kids with the whole world ahead of them trying to save a life. His right eye was swollen from the rock those kids had thrown and he slipped in some mud on the field. Chucky was a good fifty yards in front of him shouting *"Come on, come on!"* Pain screamed up his leg, but Matt ignored it. There was no time to think, no time for pain. He had to keep going.

Matt fought his way to his feet, his Chuck Taylors acting like oil slicks on the wet grass; some places still had snow. The quiet afternoon was replaced by heavy breathing, and suddenly he could hear the screaming, he remembers. Yes, screaming into the late afternoon dusk, the voice of a girl, the sound swallowed by the fog rising off the thawing New England snowpack that looked like ghosts.

They both arrive at the edge of the field where the brush and thickets met with the quick mud and reeds. The grass and buds pushing their way through the end of the snow had that delightfully bright odor of fertilized mush that only means winter is over in New England. Sweet smelling flowers and the hum of June bugs would arrive eventually, people would line up to purchase ten-dollar bleacher seats at Fenway, but not yet. No, the past winter had been particularly harsh as many New England winters are, and the thaw had been slow, dragging into mid-April.

The wind caused fresh tears to flow from Matt's swollen eye, and he rubbed them away with his sleeve.

Pretty soon they would see the bridge.

The slope comes at them fast, but they are prepared; they've run this course nearly every day for the better part of three years. Now, their feet are flying by mere muscle memory alone. He hears her again, calling out now. *She's screaming*, he thinks. *Screaming*. And then another sound, louder now. Mechanical, rumbling. Close.

Faster now, he thinks. Down the embankment, first Chucky, and then Matt. Chucky jumps down and keeps going. Matt has to slide. The clay is still frozen causing his jacket to slide up, exposing his back, scratching his flesh on the hard-exposed roots. He winces, but it doesn't matter. Just another ache to numb the other aches.

They are on their feet now.

They see the bridge in the distance, a massive structure of termite infested railroad ties bordered by chain link fence only a hundred or so feet away. They see the girl lying on her back, the train tracks so close, and they see *him,* and now they are bolting. *No!* Matt thinks, his feet fall one after the other, ignoring the agony of his left leg. And for the first time he can remember that he passes Chucky, winning a race neither want to run. He sees the boy and girl and they're closer now and the screaming.

Oh God, her screaming.

Chucky speeds up and now it is Matt who trails, falling back. His feet pump double time, but it seems like the faster he runs, the farther and farther she gets, his legs marching static in his mud-soaked sneakers. And as Chucky turns the corner disappearing around the bend, Matt hears the echoes of shrieks mixing with the chirping of blackbirds and robins, and he thinks *I couldn't stop it.*

I couldn't stop it.

I couldn't-

He wakes to the sound of sneakers squeaking on linoleum tile and looks up to see Monk, one of the others. Monk was in his late sixties and lived like a vampire, sleeping only as the sun crept through the hospital windows. He spent most mornings squeaking up and down the checkered hallway, as Barry, the night orderly snoozed behind three inches of fracture-proof plexiglass.

Breakfast is runny eggs on soggy toast, and Matt lets it sit. He would try the coffee but knew better. The shit would hang in his stomach like battery acid. Everything here tasted like chemicals. He would swear on it. Rocco, the line cook, if you could call the guy who wheels up thirty pre-made trays of food wrapped in plastic a cook, calls over.
 "Hey, Matt. Not hungry?"
 "Feel like shit," Matt groans, and he did. The nightmares always brought on insomnia, which brought on loss of appetite, which made him irritable, and so on and so on. He rubs his hands through greasy hair and lays his head on the cafeteria table.
 Outside the cafe he hears a commotion.
 "You can't do this to me!" the man screams. "You can't! You can't!"
 A gurney with a middle-aged man is quickly wheeled past the entranceway, the occupant handcuffed to the arm rail. Matt sees this, but from his angle, head on the table, the stretcher looks like a rocketship going straight down to Hell, and he thinks to himself *sure they can, buddy. Welcome to the unit.*

Part One:

August And Everything After

Chapter One

It was the rain that stopped him. It felt like a steam room as the thunderheads roared across Back Bay. It came in sheets and torrents, the wind spraying it sideways through the alleys and awkward winding streets, bouncing off of curbstones and payphone receivers, overflowing storm drains. It happened suddenly, Matt thought; the forecast hadn't called for rain initially. But there it was, drenching his khakis, his right sock sopping up puddles through a hole in the sole; he never invested in shoes that would last. Dan Simmons on Channel 7 had warned against a few showers later on in the week, but not tonight. Not now. There was even an implication that the heatwave may last through most of next week, the index stating the air quality was dangerous for the young and elderly, to avoid going out if you were prone to asthma, respiratory problems, and nausea. And for the most part he'd been correct on his assumption. The forecast was brutally accurate all week, with lows in the high nineties. But then this storm, tonight, came out of nowhere. The temperature had suddenly dropped to the mid-seventies and BANG came the thunder. It happened only twenty minutes ago, and Matt knew, with his luck, would only last another ten at best. *But this*, he thought. *This changes everything*.

BOYS, BROKEN

He stood on an inclined ledge on the sixth floor of a parking garage off of Boylston Street, his sneakers toeing the lip of the concrete, nothing but a few inches separating them from air. Slowly, he rocked back and forth and leaned over the edge. *Free fall*, he thought. This was the fourth time in seven days he had stood on this particular roof, the fourth time he had sung Tom Petty in his head. Today was supposed to be the day. But that damn rain. That, he thought, hadn't been in the plan.

Ask any psychiatrist and he'll tell you that among the patients that have seriously contemplated suicide, not necessarily the cry-for-help, bottle of Tylenol one-pill-at-a-time people, but the people who have a complacency, an almost indifferent outlook on death itself, are the people who create and ruminate on a plan to kill oneself so detailed that any micro-deviation from the plan will likely cause the person to reconsider, reschedule, or at the least, stop for the moment to get their metaphorical ducks in a row. Blueprints of self-destruction; manifestos for future ghosts. These plans had to be followed to a "T."

Matt's plan had been simple. Find the tallest public garage with roof access, get there early enough on his morning commute to not raise any suspicion from the nightwatchman or early bird joggers, and leap into the great wide open, as the song goes. It would be the quickest way, he figured, for someone without access to a firearm or strong enough pipe to swing from. Fast and sudden and without the slightest care of just how ugly anything could be. And then everything would be quiet. Everything would be still. Most importantly, everything, he knew, would be over. That was an extremely calming thought. And for the first time since he could remember, he had been at peace.

But then the sky opened and this - *this fucking rain*, he thought. It was supposed to be over. All of this. *Everything*. He felt like a thirty-something phantom, a being with no purpose trying to find a place in displacement.

Matt closed his eyes. He was unaware of it, but at that moment, he felt his legs give way and he fell onto the seat of his pants. He looked like a toddler who had an accident. His whole body collapsed with an ache that throbbed, his head a sudden migraine, stomach in knots. He tried to make it to his feet, pulling himself up by the concrete slab he had so recently been grasping. He stood, brushed his hand through his soaked hair as if he were rinsing conditioner. Once he was steady, he took one look over the lip of the roof.

The alley below was silent save for the ratatat of the raindrops pelting the dumpster of the bowling alley next to the garage. It was one of those luxury places with chic waitresses that delivered straight to your lane, balancing Coronas and Harpoon IPAs and oversized pretzels on trays to tables that always seemed to wobble a bit much. He'd been there once. Found it overpriced and boring.

A hand grasped his shoulder. He turned, startled.

"Chucky?" he almost yelped and became aware that he was staring not into the face of his pale, ginger haired friend from childhood, but that of the middle-aged nightwatchman from the lobby. Was his name Hal? Or Leonard? It was on the tip of his tongue.

"The hell you doing out in this?" the guard said. The man wore a poncho, the hood drooping over his wet mocha-colored skin, and for a second Matt couldn't believe he thought it had been his old Irish friend. Matthew's face suddenly collapsed, and if it weren't for the storm, the man would have been able to see the tears streaming down his face. "Shit, man. You...are you alright?"

Matt didn't lean so much as fall into the man's arms, embracing him in a one-way hug. His sobs turned into a barbaric heaving yawp and his entire body started to shake.

He couldn't speak.

"Damn," the guard said. "It's okay. It's gonna be okay." The man reached into the pocket of his slicker and pulled out a walkie-talkie. "Hey, Joey, I'm gonna need some help here."

And that was when Matthew Rode puked.

BOYS, BROKEN

From the moment the door shut, locked, the pale white walls staring into his eyes, a dead television set anchored to the wall hidden behind protective shatterproof glass, a lone stretcher permanently locked in an unfortunate inclined position, he knew he had made a mistake. Or maybe that was not the right word. "Mistake" conjures up feelings of accidents, mishaps, faux-pas. This was none of those things.

The emergency department was curiously empty on the Thursday morning when Matthew checked in. The admissions desks, which seemed to have gone through some recent systems upgrade, as the desks themselves were more of a series of mobile stations with attendants sitting next to laptop computers or tablets, was less of the pick-a-number deli style he was so used to. He noticed that all the desks were empty and made his way cautiously to the closest station available. A young brunette greeted him.

"Hello," she said. She was all smiles, her blonde hair pulled back into a tight bun. It would look amazing down as it would accent her high cheek bones, he thought. "How can I assist you today?"

He paused.

That was a good question.

Until only a few hours ago he had been perched above Boston's Back Bay neighborhood trying to do the math of whether or not six stories would be the correct height to jump from in order to stop the noises and nightmares, the hunger and vice. To stop everything. But he hadn't factored in the slope of the street the garage was on, or the fact that it was pouring down rain at the time (though the sun had risen hot and early, his drenched khakis and work shirt sure didn't agree), and, knowing that he, a loathsome student of numbers who didn't pass his core curriculum college courses until his fifth year didn't know if she was the correct person to ask to shed some light. But all he could come up with was, "Garage."

"Hmmm?" She asked. "Cookie, you gotta go to the parking desk to get your ticket validated."

He shook his head.

"No, I'm. What I meant to say is," he gulped. She looked into his eyes, her brow furrowed with concern.

"You okay, hon? I can get some-"

"I'm having these thoughts. Really bad thoughts," he trailed off. "I just tried to, well. I mean. It's just that-"

She maintained her smile and looked at him. His eyes drifted to her name tag (Beverly) and wondered who such a pretty and sweet girl had pissed off to be born with such a tired old name.

"Oh, of course," she said so matter-of-factly, as if he had just told her that two plus two was four. "We're here to help," she said, and he thought *Damn, you could help me by letting me back out for a smoke*. But the time for that had passed. Besides, the rain had done a number on his pack of Winstons - he imagined that if he could manage to pull them from his pocket, they would be a crumpled mess. "You've come to the right place," she finished. "Do you have your card?"

He reached into his wallet, pushed aside his credit cards, a few ATM receipts, a photo of his wife, pulled out his Blue Cross and handed it to her. "Thanks. Now I just need to get you registered. This will only take a few minutes, k hon?"

A few seconds of typing followed. She took the usual information and demographics and directed him to a seat at the triage station.

"Just sit over there. The nurse will be out shortly, sweety. A few minutes." She handed him a plastic cup of water and said, "Drink this. You look so red." She walked away and for a second, he could have sworn she glanced back at him, but he wasn't quite sure.

He sat, pulling out his worn and wet copy of *The Alchemist* from his messenger bag. He began thumbing through but some of the pages were glued together, the yellow paper damaged from the water. This, for some reason, made the situation more real, and he winced back tears.

BOYS, BROKEN

He put the book back into the satchel and sighed. He'd been involved in the healthcare industry, if that's what you would call it, for most of his professional career and knew that when the staff said it would only be a few minutes, it was better to come prepared. What was it his mother used to say that he had so clearly ignored today? Dress for rain?

―――

"Mr. Rode," the nurse said as she entered. The woman was a little older, maybe late thirties, but she had a comforting smile and bright auburn curls that made her look ten years younger. Her lab coat was covering both a set of navy scrubs underneath and, he thought he could see as she leaned over, maybe a tee-shirt under those? He noticed that there were layers of rubber bands doubled over the arms of her cat's eye glasses, which, it seemed, prevented them from slipping down her face. Quite an impressive feat. He would have to jot that one down for future use on muggy days. Her sneakers were double knotted, laced across, instead of criss-cross style, and her topaz pinky ring had a-

"Mr Rode?"

Startled. He had been caught. Was he not paying attention? Did he miss something she said?

Oh God, did he say something out loud?

Of course, you did, Pukeface, he heard a child say somewhere else.

"Yes?" he managed to whisper.

She was looking at him through those wide bifocal lenses, their glare off the computer screen disappearing her eyes behind reflections of his patient chart in mirror image.

"It says here you feel depressed," she paused. "You are having thoughts. Suicidal thoughts?"

The way she said that last word was cold, clinical. It stung hearing it aloud.

She continued. "And that you attempted to take your life." She typed; her fingers click-click-clicked like a spectator in the cramped room. "Have you always had a history of depression? Is that correct?"

Again, clinical, but at least she was honest. Though it wasn't her fault. This was her job. If anything, this was without a doubt his fault. He was an adult (as far as the voting age, drinking age, and selective-service were concerned) and entirely capable of making adult decisions (his wife and friends could certainly argue against *that* point, especially considering the present circumstances). She was only doing her job, he thought. But hearing those words just seemed so...what? What did it seem? She didn't mean any harm and may honestly, though highly unlikely, he figured, actually care. More than not, she was working an uncharacteristically slow morning shift at Boston's largest trauma center. She was just getting her facts straight.

"Depression, yes. I guess it would be depression," he paused. "Though not diagnosed, officially." He combed his hair back with one hand, the hair he got from his father's side of the family, thick and rich with auburn and with no evidence of a receding line. He had a terrible headache that pulsed with the stale bright lights reflecting off the tile. A headache ironically the side effect of downing half a bottle of extra strength ibuprofen before attempting his leap of faith. You know - to really make sure it counted. Of course, this was to no avail, or else he wouldn't be where he currently was, having this current conversation, with this current nurse, this current headache. No, Matthew Rode thought, now, whatever was left of those pills were dripping down the sides of a nightwatchman's poncho. It was almost funny. Your liver may very well be fucked in twenty years, perhaps sooner than that. But you'll have plenty of time to deal with the throbbing for now.

"And suicidal..." he trailed off again.

Ha, Ha, Ha! Matt. You gimp. You waste. He heard the group of voices chanting, chanting from somewhere. The waiting room? *Gonna get you new kid. Been waiting all year.*

He closed his eyes tightly and held his breath.

The nurse stopped typing and looked up from her screen. Right at him.

"Sorry," he continued. "Ideations, I guess? Thoughts? Is that the correct way to word it?" His left hand was shaking rapidly, sweat beaded on his brow. "I just want to get it right," he continued. "This being my first time."

"Right, sure. Of course. And are you still wanting to harm yourself?" She took a pen out of her bun and began chewing on it. That was another good question. The staff here could all make decent replacements as judges on *Jeopardy!* She continued to type as he answered.

"Yes," the words almost swallowed. "I mean no."

He fidgeted in his seat. His right knee bouncing like he was constantly playing hi-hat to a cymbal that wasn't there. He noticed that her typing had sped up. "Not now, I guess," he added. "I don't think."

He let out a long sigh, knelt forward, and sunk his head into his hands. The ache of his throbbing migraine was really doing a number on his ability to concentrate. He began to quietly sob.

"Mr. Rode."

"Please, call me Matthew. Or Matt," he said, wiping his face. "The only people that call me 'Mister' are bill collectors."

"Okay, Matthew," she smiled. He looked at her glasses again, this time noticing the tortoise shell pattern of the frames, just like the ones Chucky used to wear when they were kids. "Now, we get to the tough questions, okay? Standard operating procedure and everything, pretty milquetoast. But I have to ask, okay?"

"Yes. Sure," he nodded.

"You made a big decision, a tough decision coming here. I know you aren't feeling your best right now. But I need to ask. Do you feel safe?" She continued. "I am required by state law to ask, 'do you feel safe?', but seriously." She moved her hand away from the keyboard and for a second, he thought she was going to reach out and touch his hand but didn't. "Are you having any thoughts of harming yourself? Others?"

That was the question, wasn't it? Final Jeopardy, and all that.

"Not," he began. "Not others, no." Her eyes turned into daggers, and for a moment he thought she would have something to say. But her hand clicking off checkboxes with the mouse was the only reply. "And 'yes' to the first part, I think. About safety." She began typing again.

"That's fine," she answered. "And, sorry to backtrack, but I need as much information as possible to make sure we follow the right guidelines. Procedures. Right?"

"I guess?" He replied.

"So, besides the thoughts, you said you made an attempt."

"Correct."

"And this was, when? Today?" She asked. "Last week?"

He shook his head. "Last night. Or, technically this morning. Around 4:00 AM."

"Okay," she said for the umpteenth time. "And the method?"

"Method?"

She took a sip of her coffee, put the cup down next to the keyboard. The aroma mixed with the stale alcohol scent of the hospital didn't sit well with his stomach. Perhaps this was a mistake? "The method that you were going to-"

From the waiting room he could hear the giggling, louder now. Louder.

He waved her off.

"Right. Gotcha." Matt sat up in his chair, which was hell on his back after decades of slouching. "Well, I was going to jump."

Jump. With that *leg?* another kid's voice said.

"Jump," she repeated. The keys clicked and clacked and he felt the mechanical noises reverberate in his head again and the laughter, the *laughter just grew and grew and* –

"From where?"

"Is the location really that important?" his voice raising.

"If you think it is, yes."

He sighed again.

"There's this garage near a bar I used to go to."

"Garage," she said. "A parking garage?"

"Yeah, over in Back Bay." He's practically shouting now. "It's public. Twenty-four hours. Has roof access." He stopped, and the nurse looked as if she saw something in his eye, something he was trying to grasp on to.

Come on, Matty. Come, on. Jump, jump, jump!

"Do you hear kids?" he asked, loudly.

"Excuse me?"

Like that, was nothing there.

"Never mind," his head shakes. "Sorry. Anyway," he continued, softer. "I was up there this morning, had it all planned out. And the fucking storm comes in and I freak. This guy shows up, some employee. I break down in front of him. This total stranger. And he drops me off here. Imagine that, right?"

There is a long pause.

"Anything else from your history that we may have overlooked?"

He thought for a moment.

"There was an accident. When I was younger." Her typing picked up speed, stopped, began again. And stopped. In between these intervals, she would occasionally look over her frames to Matt's direction, like she was eyeing the dessert menu at an all-night diner, and then begin typing again. "There's a steel rod in my leg," he finished.

She was a fast typer, he thought. He could only manage 40 words per minute on a good day. Although he grew up in the age of the internet, in between the millennials and the X-er's, he never landed the skill of typing without looking at the screen. Most of the time he only used two fingers. And if he made a mistake, well -

The phone next to her computer rang and she picked it up.

"Yes. We're ready," she answered. "Yes. Yes. Mmhmm. Yes, Section 12. Thanks."

Matt's pocket buzzed. Fuck, he thought. In the chaotic mess that was last night he had forgotten to call in to work letting them know he would be "out sick," which he thought was kind of funny; not "ha-ha" funny, but you know. He glanced at the clock on the wall and decided it was weird for his supervisor to only be texting him given that he was already over two hours late. He reached into his pocket and came another regret; he really wished he had that last Winston before coming in here. He found his phone and tugged it out of his pocket.

The notification screen had a small smiling slot machine emoticon announcing "Hurry! Your Free Spins Bonus Will Expire 2-Nite!"

Words escaped him.

He needed to set the damn notifications off. His wife was always asking why he always had to get office emails on the weekend, and he would always reply that it was "just the nature of a busy office, being tethered 24/7" when he was really playing Pharoah's Fool's Gold on the shitter.

He opened his web browser and started seeing if any groundbreaking events had happened the night before, if the apocalypse had occurred, nuclear war (something his cellphone slot machine notification made him highly doubt). Then it hit him. What did the nurse say into the phone? Besides a lot of yeses, he thought, she mentioned something about Section 12. Was that it? He typed it into his search engine and clicked on the first link:

Section 12: Emergency restraint and hospitalization of persons posing risk of serious harm by reason of mental illness

BOYS, BROKEN

Section 12. (a) Any physician who is licensed pursuant to section 2 of chapter 112 or qualified psychiatric nurse mental health clinical specialist authorized to practice as such under regulations promulgated pursuant to the provisions of section 80B

All at once he really needed that cigarette. He shoved his phone back into his pocket when, instantly, it began ringing again, only this time it didn't stop. It was a call, he thought, and given the awkward angle he was sitting in, realized his hand was hopelessly stuck. And now here he was, thrashing about in a triage chair while this nurse kept her eyes fixed on the computer screen.

Now it's work, he thought. It's work and Joanna has finally gone to Debbie in Human Resources because Matt was out sick again and he would surely be fired. To hell with it. He would be shit-canned.

His fingers found his phone and managed to squeeze it to the tip of his jeans pocket when it slipped and fell to the floor. He could see the "Missed Call" notification, but it wasn't from work. It was from Carol, the divorcee from across the street that sat for his son, Gabriel. His heart sank. A call from Carol was never good news because either she was sick (bad) or Gabriel was (worse). He bent over to reach for the phone when a meaty palm gripped his shoulder and he froze.

"Shit!" Allie Rode said. "Oh shit. No, Oh FUCK!"

Her empty Nissan was quiet save for the soothing state of affairs coming from NPR's Morning Edition, and there was no one there to scold her.

"I can't…" she continued. "I just can't EVEN!"

Some blue shirt in a VW Rabbit had cut three lanes across I-93 North and would have cut directly into her driver's side panel if she hadn't slammed on her brakes. The result was threefold. (1) The large Iced French Vanilla from Dunkin's sloshed onto her (2) closing agreements she was driving up to goddam Wilmington, causing her to (3) get rear-ended by an ancient Crown Victoria. She could tell from the thud that there was some damage, if only minor. But Matt was still going to be pissed. They had just finished paying off the lease, and now the little Nissan in cherry red (her choice) was theirs. No more payments, hooray! But that was ten-minutes-ago's problem, now. Currently, Allie Rode had to pull over, get some info, and get to that closing.

She pulled to the breakdown lane and remembered that yes, hadn't she once owned a great Crown Vic, or something of the sort? Wait, yes. She had a Mercury Grand Marquis from the late eighties. Same concept really. Combine a couch and a tank and you're good to go, minus the nine miles to the gallon it got on a good day downhill. She loved her Merc, silver gray save for one blue side-panel on the passenger side. Bitch was a tank. But what she knew then was what she knew now. When you were in an accident with a tank, even one in bumper-to-bumper going 25 or less, you lose.

She opened the glove compartment, ignored the half-pack of stale Winston's, also ignoring the once six-pack now three-pack of multicolored Bic lighters. She could use that against Matt tonight if he was upset about the car, she thought. When he's angry about this fender bender, I could bring up the smoking. *How come you're still sneaking them? How come?* But again, that was for Later Allie. Current Allie had to find The Papers, as her father would have called them, stressing their importance so you could actually hear the capitalization in his voice. Registration, insurance, the like. She ruffled between the forest of extra Dunkin Donuts napkins and tissues.

"Shit," she doubled down. How come you always have what you need when you don't want it, and can never find what you need when you do? She continued, her hand foraging until-

"Yes!"

She sat up, looked over herself in the mirror, and noticing her hair and makeup looked fine (fine enough for a roadside confrontation

BOYS, BROKEN

with a whoziwhatsit- she would no doubt pull off in Reading or Woburn to give herself the good once over before heading on to the closing- but for now this was fine.

The door opened and she immediately regretted wearing her camisole. It was muggy, as late Boston summers tend to be, and though she had her blazer hanging in the back seat from those handles she never really understood the use for, she worried that she may have visible sweat stains once she arrived at the meeting.

The Vic's owner was aware of none of this. From the looks of it, he didn't seem to be aware of anything at all. From her vantage point, it appeared to Allie Rode that this gentleman, (this *older* gentleman, she thought), was about to fall asleep.

"Excuse me, sir?" she asked.

Head bobbing. Up. Down. Up. Down.

She knocked on his window.

Up. Down. Up. Down.

She noticed a box of tissues in the rear window, the kind that seem to be in the rear window of every Vic or Merc - which always puzzled her. She had purchased hers from her roommate's father back in college - a steal at $1,100. And she would swear on a stack of pancakes that her window would have a similar box, too.

"Sir!" She slammed her hand on the hood. Jolted, he now sat up.

"What? What's it?" he asked.

His head, now awoke, had stopped nodding up and down and was now doing that fake-it-till-you-make-it dance of rolling side to side at odd angles, will he/won't he?

The traffic on 93 ebbed and crawled. Allie noticed some folks staring as gawkers are wont to do.

"Tired. So tired," he slurred.

On the passenger seat, she noticed a Gillette razor hat and figured the guy might be coming off third shift, hell, maybe a double, which would certainly explain the grogginess. Matty, she remembered, had to work third shift at the call center *and* first at the hospital while Allie had been on maternity leave. He averaged about four hours' sleep most nights, and that was only when baby Gabe had let him sleep. Still, her empathy didn't mean she wasn't pissed as all hell at this guy who was clearly fucking up both of their days.

After a tedious twenty minutes of back and forth, Allie Rode was finally able to get the driver's name (David Dirbuck) and insurer (the one with the cavemen commercials that Matty found just delightful). When she returned to the Nissan, she checked herself out in the mirror and hated what she saw. The mid-morning humidity had done a number on her hair. *Maybe I should reschedule*, she thought. She reached into her purse and unearthed her cell. It had been on silent (not vibrate, *silent*, which Matty would give her an earful for that later). Looking at her home screen, she froze. There were seven missed calls in the past nineteen minutes, all from the same 617 number. Normally she didn't pick up calls from a number she didn't know; if you were friends, you were already in each others' phones. And in this day and age, who even knew each other's phone numbers? Hell, she didn't even know her husband's phone number. But a stranger who calls *seven times*?

She hit the callback button. It rang twice and picked up. Her heart sank when she heard the automated switchboard for Suffolk County Hospital.

Yes, she thought. *I am definitely going to reschedule.*

Chapter Two

When he was younger, around eleven or twelve, Matt Rode had been in an accident. It's one of life's great mysteries, how the minor things in our lives - an uncapped pen ruining a dress shirt leading to a day at the laundromat where you meet your future wife, or the old friend you hadn't seen in years and always wondered how she was doing winds up on the same subway car, and you discover she just moved into the neighborhood you recently moved out of - can change everything.

Matt's life was changed by a game of tag.

He had just moved to Reedy Pond, a small suburb of Boston, from the even smaller suburbs of Providence with just a week left in the school year when he met an affectionate group of kids that would eventually refer to themselves as The Gang, a sort-of mix between The Loser's Club and The Goonies, sans the supernatural aspects of the former or the Inspector Gadget-like gizmos and booby traps of the latter. The group was comprised of Chucky and his younger sister Catherine Dawson - but she always went by Cat ("Only my grandparents call me Catherine"), and twins Tommy and Eddie O'Connell. Chucky was short for fourth grade and Cat, though one grade younger, was an inch-and-a-half taller than him. They both had hair as red as bricks. The twin boys lived on Tyler Street near the aptly named Tyler Street Bridge, an old wooden expanse positioned above the railroad heading to northern New England, or south to Boston. The bridge itself and surrounding acre of gravel and dirt was condemned and chained off, but it never stopped the kids from building fortresses or finding buried treasure in one of its many surrounding thickets. When referring to themselves on the rare occasion that they did, it was always as The Gang, in capital letters.

The day he was first introduced to The Gang was gorgeous. Blue sky, seventy-three degrees, slight breeze in the morning air. He was heading up to the schoolyard on his BMX to check out the new playground that was just finished the week before. It was a new wooden structure that spanned a great deal of field at Reedy Pond Elementary, full of tall slides, high steeples, and monkey bars. The main portion of the structure was a huge house style building about twenty feet tall housing a twirly-slide of yellow PVC, fireman's pole, and a vertical tunnel with rectangular footholds to climb up and down. A flexible bridge made of tires and chain spanned fifteen feet to a second, smaller structure that veered off to the monkey bars. The entire border of the playground was encased in railroad ties, the ground a layer of tons and tons of pea-stone. It had been funded by the PTA the previous year through various bake sales and knitting drives and was erected by a local contractor and some parent volunteers. Jack Dawson, the father of Chucky and Cat, was the one to install the finishing touch on top of the steeple - an old-fashioned rooster weather vane.

Matt hadn't made any friends as of late, it being the first week of summer, so when he parked his Haro next to the pile of bikes in the trees at the foot of the school's baseball field, and heard the happy sounds of kids shouting, he immediately became intrigued. He snuck a glance from behind the pile of bikes and saw a group of kids playing, well, something.

But what were they playing, exactly?

It reminded him of tag or hide-and-seek. Someone was definitely "It," but what confused him was that no one was hiding, and no one was running. It wasn't Freeze Tag, or Television. The twins, he could see, had scaled their way to the top of the tall spire. Another kid - he had met him in the two days he spent in math class the week before school got out, thought his name might be Chuck? - was dangling from the monkey bars upside down, using an extra bar as a catch for his feet. The girl was walking along the railroad-tie boundary of the playground, arms outstretched as if she were a gymnast on a balance beam. Matt could hear the shouting clearer, now.

"Can't get me!" the red head boy said.

"Can so!" the girl hollered. But instead of darting for him, she continued to inch forward. One foot. Then the next. Then another step. Then another. The twins were cracking up. Matt was confused. Why didn't she just go out and get him? The monkey bars were only a dozen steps away at most. Why wasn't she attacking? He followed up this thought with another and made the bravest decision the new kid can make.

"Hey!" he called out from under the pines. This action startled the kids, who began looking in different directions as if they were spooked by some Ghost of Playground's Past. But it was Tommy who spotted Matt from atop the spire.

"Who goes thar?" Tommy shouted in his best pirate.

"It's the new kid from Walnut Street," Chucky replied. "I saw the U-Haul outside the other day. The Sterling's old place." Matt started running towards them, his Red Sox tee-shirt billowing in the breeze.

"Yeah?" Eddie asked.

"Guess so," Matt answered, panting. He was a little thick for his age and the sprint across the field in the heat did him no favors. "What are you guys," he breathed in heavily. "Up to?"

Chucky - who had until this point still been hanging upside down - carefully swiveled himself over and dropped onto his feet. "'No Touch Ground Tag.' Or 'N.T.G.T' for short."

Matt was silent.

"What," he began, "does that even mean?"

Eddie answered, "No. Touch. Ground. Tag." The way he said it, dotting each word with a capital letter, Matt could tell they always said this phrase with such emphasis. "What are you, slow? You can't touch the ground, newbie. It's in the name. It's - it's - it's -"

"Lava," Matt finished. "It's like regular tag but on steroids!"

"It's like regular tag, but on steroids!" Matt peered over in the direction of the doubling voice to see that it was the girl. He smiled.

"Anyway, that's what we used to call it. Lava. Back home." He immediately thought of Bob and Jay and Steve and Nate, all his buddies back in Rhode Island, and he wondered if they were at the beach, or playing fort, or going to see the PawSox this weekend. He felt a twinge in his stomach. "I'm Matt Rode, by the way. Matty."

"Chucky."

"Eddie."

"Tommy."

"Catherine. But don't you call me that or I'll - "

"She'll kick your ass!" Chucky finished and smiled. "Call her Cat, and you'll have no problems."

They were all smiles now.

"Alright, breaks over," Chucky said. "Cat's still 'It,' so on the count of ten, let's go!"

Nice to meet you, Matt thought. And it *was* nice. He had wanted so hard to make friends, to not be so alone this summer. He was still pissed at his dad for getting that promotion over in the city, uprooting Matt from his life back home, moving up 95. He figured he'd spend the better part of the summer listening to Siamese Dream and playing Genesis, but now it seemed like things were looking up. Things were -

"Hey," Chucky called. "You playing?"

"Yeah," Matt said. "Yeah, totally. Sure!"

"Cause you're on the ground."

Matt looked at his feet, saw that he was standing in the gravel, and immediately hopped onto a railroad-tie. Chucky winked.

"Don't worry. You're not out," he said. "Everyone gets one."

BOYS, BROKEN

They played all morning, broke for lunch, and met back up at 12:30. They ditched their bikes in the bushes as they did before, only this time, as they returned to the playground there was a small group of younger kids, mostly girls, hanging out by the swings. They looked to Matt to be around Cat's age, and this idea was confirmed when a lanky brunette covered in freckles shouted "Hiya, toots!"

Cat turned to The Gang.

"That's Nickie Lester and some of her friends. I told them to meet us here, if that's okay."

The boys looked at each other and then to Chucky. Though he was new to the group, Matt could tell that if they had a leader - whatever a leader of boys *could* be - Chucky was it.

"If they want," he said, paused, then shouted loud enough for the girls to hear, "but we're not going to go easy on you just cause you're smaller!"

At this, both Tommy and Eddie laughed. This made Chucky crack a wide grin.

"Who is?" Cat replied. "I'm taller than you, ass-hat!"

It was at this point that they all erupted, Chucky included. After a few moments to contain themselves, Chucky said, "Come on, guys. Are we gonna play or what?" And they did. For hours they climbed the sides of the castle, dangled from the monkey bars, and tried to out best each other with the most creative hiding spot. Matt found he was quite good at standing on the swings and trapezing himself between the bunch. The "lava" they had to avoid was a layer of pea stone, pebbles small enough that, if one were to fall from an average height, could certainly make you lose your wind, but would provide just enough cushion as to not break a rib. Of course, if you were doing something stupid, like Eddie was now - scaling the roof of the domed-spiral slide - if he lost his grip, well -

But the Gang did not think like that. Kids never do. Kids, especially *summer* kids, *play*. Thinking, worrying, making big decisions; these were problems for grownups. And though the word subconscious would not enter their vocabulary exams for a few more years the kids had some deeper knowing that someday, yes, they would grow up and have responsibilities and bills and lose that unmistakable awe - the magic that was summer. But for now -

"You're out!" Tommy shouted at Cat. She had been attempting her balance beam act once more and lost her footing. She went down onto the pebbles hard. She made a "Eesh!" sound but she didn't cry, though her knee had been skinned. The wound was caked with dust and pebbles. When you were "out" you had to go sit on the benches at the baseball diamond. Most of Cat's friends, being younger and less agile, had already taken up most of the spots, but Eddie was there, too. He was tagged out by Charlie Thorn, one of the 3rd graders, when he had tried to leapfrog over him on one of the platforms near the monkey bars. It hadn't worked. Cat marched over to the bench and found her seat, and Matt noticed how absolutely pretty she looked in the afternoon sun. This thought was enough of a distraction for him to miss the hand-off between the swing's chains and go ass-over-teakettle directly onto his shoulder. The sound of his body hitting the ground made an ugly thud.

The pain was bright and sharp, his neck and collarbone throbbing. His head was spinning all around. The last two players, Chucky and Tommy, darted off their obstacles and ran to their new friend who just ate ground.

"Time!" Tommy hollered, as if more concerned with the game. After a moment, the rest of the kids greeted them.

"Shit, Matt," Eddie said.

"You okay?" Tommy added.

Chucky put up his arms in a hold-back gesture, then knelt.

"Give him some room, guys," Chucky said.

Matt had no idea if he was okay. Embarrassed? Yes. Hurt? Sure! He knew that all he could see were stars and that the wind had been knocked right out of him. He gasped.

"Can he breathe?" Nicky asked. The twins bent down and attempted to pick him up.

BOYS, BROKEN

"No!" Cat shouted. "On *Rescue 911* they always say not to move someone. If he has a broken bone or something, it could go to his heart and he could *die!*"

Great, Matt thought. Now I'm going to die. *Fourth Grader Killed While Playing Tag.* Such a lame headline. He could think of the Channel 6 news reporter on the scene: *"Well, Bob and Diane, we have a shocking tale this afternoon. Matt Rode had moved to a new town and had just started making friends. But that was before he fell victim to 'The Game.' Film at eleven."* This would no doubt be followed by lightning strikes and an orchestral dun-dun-Dun for added effect.

"You kids okay?"

The voice came from behind; it was husky, like that of a man who spent his lunch breaks chain smoking Parliaments, chewing on the recessed filter. Everyone, sans Matt, jumped.

It was a man, probably late twenties, in cut-off jeans and a Red Sox hat. He was holding a leash that was attached to the collar of the biggest Saint Bernard Matt had ever seen, a thick string of monster drool dangled from its lips.

"Oh...kay," Matt managed.

The man with the dog squatted, touched Matt's shoulder.

"Ye-Shhhh," Matt winced.

"Hurt?" he asked.

"Only a li - little," Matt stammered. But this was a lie. Inside he was screaming. So much pain. Tears were welling in his eyes, but he fought to hold them back. This was his first day playing with these kids, the only ones he knew. He didn't want to come off as a baby. What if they wouldn't let him back in?

"Yeah," the man said. "Might be a fracture. Best idea is we get you to the hospital. Gotta have that looked at."

"The hospital?" Matt asked, panicked.

"The emergency room and everything?" added Tommy. "Kid, that's awesome!"

"My house is just down the road," the man said. "We can call your mom and have her come get you."

"Call my mom, sure," Matt said, and then stopped. "Shit. She won't have the car. My dad had to take it to the station and took the subway into work this morning."

"I'll talk to her," the man said. "We'll figure something out. But we need to get you looked at ASAP, right? Come on."

"Okay." Matt reached out with his good arm and the man lifted him up.

"Name's Sandy," the man said. "And this is Bruce." He pets the dog's head. The dog returned this favor with more drool.

"Matt."

He said bye to the other kids. Chucky promised to store Matt's bike in his garage (*You wouldn't want the eighth graders stealing it*, were his words).

Sandy led the dog, who was surprisingly gentle for his size, back to his home which was indeed right down the street. For the second time that day Matt decided that, besides the whole arm thing, just maybe things were looking up. Less than an hour later, he would change his mind.

———

The phone rang twice before Marcia Rode answered.

"Hello?" She could hear moaning in the background.

"Hello, Ma'am. My name is Sandy Els. I live over on Maplethorpe. I have your son with me." Sandy realized that this sounded more like a hostage negotiation. "I'm sorry. I meant to say there was an accident. He fell and we should get him to the hospital."

"He *fell?*" she had asked loudly into the phone. "What do you mean he fell?" She was nearly shouting.

"Yes, Ma'am," Sandy had said. "He was playing with some kids. Up by the school, that's where I found him. I can bring him by."

"Of course," she said without thinking. Then, Marcia paused. *What am I doing?* she thought. *How do you know he isn't a rapist? Some sort of pervert? You don't even know if he's telling the truth -*

"Hi, Ma!" Matt called out in the background. For a moment, her fears quelled. "We'll be right over to pick you up."

"Ok, hun" she said warily. "Just give me ten minutes or so to get myself together. We're still unpacking, and I haven't found the Important Files. I need to get the insurance."

She said this last part matter-of-factly, but what she really needed was a breath mint and some clothes. She had turned her evening glass of wine into an afternoon glass of wine, and a gin and tonic. She was wearing a bra and white cotton panties. For some reason, she always cleaned the house in her underwear. It was just easier that way. Less of a mess. And with the kid off playing and discovering new things, and her stuck alone all day unpacking from their move three weeks ago, she figured no one would mind. Hell, he'd be out long enough for her to enjoy a nice cold G&T.

Matt and Sandy picked up Marcia Rode twenty minutes later and though upset about the emergency room fee, she was glad that this stranger had been available to assist. Lord knows her husband wouldn't. She was wearing a low-cut blouse that showed off more cleavage than she probably should be, but Sandy didn't seem to mind. At first glance she was taken aback by just how damn handsome this young man was. She listened with quiet intent when he explained who he was and how he found her son, but all she could think of was *You look just like my type*. And though she never rode in cars with men she didn't know (especially a man as young as Sandy), she figured she could chalk it up that this was one of those emergency situations where fate kind of drops all the puzzle pieces into your lap, some connected, and you just go with it until you figure the rest out.

They drove out of the neighborhood and onto Main Street, which was a misnomer. Sure, back in the glory days of Ike and JFK the shops and storefronts would have been packed at this time of day.

But the new strip mall shopping center in Burlington had driven away most of the foot traffic. Sure, there were the window shoppers and townies and regulars, but not enough to cause any sort of delay, so the ride through town was easy enough.

They turned up Prospect Hill and headed towards Green Street, Matt sitting in the center of the backseat, as he didn't want the shoulder strap across his collar, and he didn't want to lean against the window. Not the safest, sure, but easier on the pain for now. His entire body ached with electric pain. He remembered reading about a man who had nerve damage from an accident and told horror stories of living in constant anguish. What if he had that? But no, it was probably just the stress. He wasn't paying attention to what Sandy and his mother were talking about but could see that she kept leaning over in his direction.

Marcia and Donald Rode had been married for fourteen years, got pregnant with Matt two years in, and could count on one hand the times they "had a night to themselves" since. A mid-level investment banker, most nights, Donald Rode would be stuck working late hours on State Street, and like most recent nights, Marcia would find herself falling asleep alone in a new house, an empty glass of wine or four on her night stand, her mind reliving her prom night after-party with Frankie Marsh - how Frankie's hands were both *Russian* and *Roman* - how he kissed her neck in a way that was so soft yet determined, feeling the soft scratch of his stubble and smelling his aftershave - feeling his inner thigh and then running her hand up his rental tux pant leg and thinking *Yes! Yes! I'm ready* - knew that he was the one, that he would *always* be the one for her, and her hand would stray down towards the belt of her panties and just slowly start to rub until she slept.

And now, Matt could see that his mother's hand was slowly running up Sandy's leg, in those oddly colored acid-wash cut-offs. Sandy didn't say anything about it, but he also didn't move her hand away. Matt didn't know exactly what was happening, but it didn't make him feel good. In fact, he felt awful.

BOYS, BROKEN

They began to merge onto I-95 when Matt noticed the Crown Vic in the right lane. The driver was an old blue-hair moving dangerously slow.

"Merge!" Sandy said. This must have excited Marcia, because now, so focused on this fling of infidelity, she hadn't seen that she was being watched, that Matt saw that her hand was now placed right *there* and still Sandy wasn't doing anything about it. She squeezed.

"Come on, merge!" Sandy yelled, this time meaning it.

"Mom?"

Their car was running out of lane.

"It's okay, hon. Just some toots who doesn't know what she's - "

"Move!" Sandy yelled. Again, honking. This time he grabbed Marcia's hand and brushed it aside. The road was forking narrow and Sandy made a decision that was unexpected - instead of cutting into traffic forcing the cars in the right lane into a Darwinian exercise of slam on the brakes or perish, Sandy cut *right* and gunned the car into the breakdown lane, trying to go around the Vic.

"What are you -?" Marcia started, but that was all that came.

What the lovers in the front seat had failed to notice was the broken-down tractor-trailer in the breakdown lane directly in front of them. Matt, who had been holding onto the buckles of the side seat belts like some kind of nylon handlebars, screamed.

They say that everything gets really slow when you are facing death in the face, that time itself seems to pause. But for Matt, this wasn't the case. He could see the truck, could see what was immediately about to happen, and attempted to prepare for the worst, though this being 1994, when passenger airbags were still a paid option for most new cars - non-existent in the early-eighties mid-size sedan he was currently a passenger of - he thought to himself *Go limp, you must go limp, you must -*

And then everything went dark.

Chapter Three

The voice was deep. "Mr. Rode?" He turned expecting to see a doctor or male nurse in scrubs. Instead he saw a hulk of a man in a neat gray suit - not certain of the designer, but it didn't look cheap. Definitely something you would go into the city for, and not, say, the Square One Mall. "I'd like you to step this way, if you could."

Matt was still shaken from when this guy had grabbed him. He knelt, collected his bag and phone.

"Of course," Matt said. "Are you a doc-"

"You'll just need to come with me. Right this way, Mr. Rode." He led Matt through a series of doors and halls that seemed a maze he couldn't tell if a mile long, or merely feet. They arrived at a set of double doors. The man held up his ID badge and pressed it against a sensor on the wall. It beeped and Matt heard the *click* of the doors unlock. Matt had a similar system at work.

"And just into this room here," the man said. It looked like any normal hospital exam room - there was a bed, a sink, various trashcans and sharps bins, posters on the wall for vision, Tips on Quitting Smoking Today. Matt took a seat on the bed.

"My name's Jerry. I'm with hospital security, and I wanted to say, you are doing the right thing checking yourself in here, let me tell you."

BOYS, BROKEN

Of course, that's what you think, Jerry, Matt thought. *You're the man with the gun.*

"And let me add," he continued, "that while I commend you for being proactive - I mean you *don't* want to see the kinds of people who get dragged in here every single day from the cops - the homeless, the users - *those* people are just - I dunno." Jerry shakes his head. "I also need to inform you that you are now considered to be a Section 12. Do you know what that means?"

Twenty minutes ago, Matt would have said no. But now -

"I can't leave," Matt mumbled.

"Please speak up, Mr. Rode. I need to make sure you understand your rights."

"My rights?" he asked, more to himself. He looked down at his patient wristband, and eight-digit medical record number listed and thought, *who decided I was 22800224?* He sighed. "I'm not allowed to leave according to the law. Since I am here under my own will I have given up my right to leave the hospital until the psychiatrist agrees. Is that close?"

Jerry nodded.

"Close enough." Matt wanted to add that he knew they also thought he was crazy but thought that might be uncouth. "Now, another nurse will be coming pretty soon. Then a doc. They'll take some labs, ask you a few questions, easy peasy - lemon squeezy."

Matt's grandfather, who bragged about killing the "Chinks in Oki" would have changed the last part to "Japan-eezy."

Jerry continued. "And then the doc and the team will be able to come up with a course of action."

Jerry opened a drawer near the hospital bed and took out a clear plastic bag and an opaque one that could only be described as a trash bag with labels. The clear one had something in it. "Put these on," Jerry said. "They're like scrubs." He tossed the opaque bag to him. "This one is for your personal effects: cellphone, clothes."

Matt took off his messenger bag that contained his dress shirt, headphones, and paperback. Besides his wife and son, this was his life and it fit into a canvas bag he purchased online with an overdrafted credit card. He placed it on the floor and emptied everything into the dark trash bag. Jerry was about to leave the room, then reached into another drawer. He tossed another clear, shrink-wrapped package to Matt. They were socks with no-slip bottoms.

"I almost forgot," Jerry said. "We need your shoes and laces, too."

Matty wouldn't get to play any more games of No Touch Ground Tag that summer. Besides his dislocated shoulder (Sandy had been wrong about the collar bone, amongst other things), he didn't wake up for two weeks. Among his injuries were a broken nose, four contused ribs, the aforementioned shoulder, and the biggie - he had fractured his left femur. He was sent airborne when the truck and his car collided, which made his trajectory just shy of heading up and through the roof; the only thing that stopped him was the opposite path of the combined weight of two adults and vehicle chairs collapsing back on him simultaneously, snapping his leg and burying his head into the car's roof. He wouldn't wake up for weeks.

The passengers in the front also had a pretty bad day. His mother had most of the car's engine block end up in her lap, like some hot robotic-child asking Mrs Claus where the Big Guy went off to. She suffered second degree burns to her legs that were so bad, the dead nerves masked the pain of the crush injuries to her pelvis and lower spine. Marcia Rode would never walk again.

Sandy, who had not been wearing a seatbelt at the time of the crash because it probably made the hand job a bit more pleasing, was thrust into the steering column, collapsing his ribcage and most of his internal organs. He died almost instantly. Quite a way to start your summer vacation.

What he would learn later is that the car had collided with the semi going upwards of sixty miles per hour. The truck, a large refrigerated unit, was transporting cases of ice cream and milk from a local dairy and had blown the treads off its front passenger side tire. The driver of the truck and a roadside mechanic were busy leaning against the cab, ripping butts and shooting the shit when the sedan came barreling towards them. There was no time to beep the horn. The car collided and became a crumpled mass, the road puddled with a pink mix of dairy and blood, both souring sticky in the warm summer afternoon.

EMTs arrived at the scene after a delay of fifteen minutes, due in part to the odd location on the highway where the collision occurred, which bottlenecked the traffic back for miles. They could tell there was at least one DOA just by looking at the accordion it appeared someone was trying to drive, but once they saw Marcia's arm dangling out of the passenger side window through a cloud of smoke, they realized there could be more victims. They needed a med-flight and the jaws of life fast. It was like Matt had won the shit lottery. Your first chopper flight and car wreck in the same day.

Both Matt and his mother were evacuated to Suffolk County Hospital. Matt had a round of four surgeries on his leg. Marcia's first week at the hospital was a series of back-to-back work focusing on her crushed pelvis, mostly. While Matt was in his coma, the doctors began Marcia's skin grafts, which were difficult to say the least, as the best areas to collect from had already been cooked in the accident. In the end, they wound up taking from the smalls of her back and buttocks. When all was said and done, Marcia Rode would have to accept she wouldn't be entering any swimsuit competitions for the next hundred or so years.

Matt awoke. It was night. The hospital bed smelled like plastic. His leg throbbed, he thought he could feel his veins pulsating. He was thirsty and needed a drink. All these thoughts. All at the same time.

A nurse walked by his door, stopped, and looked in.

"Well looky here," she said. "Rip Van Winkle himself. You took a really, *really* long nap, kiddo."

He wished he could rub the sleep from his eyes.

"Wa...water," he said.

"Oh, of course," said the nurse. "Yes. And I'll get some ice chips for your throat. You sound so sore." She placed her hand softly on his.

"Mmmhmm," he whispered, but that was an understatement. It felt impossible to speak. Every word scraped his larynx like a box of nails that were on fire. The nurse turned to leave but Matt tried to speak again. She leaned in.

"Sorry, sweetie, I didn't catch that. One more time."

He gulped and took a breath. Grimacing, he managed two words. "How long?"

The nurse looked at him with eyes that seemed full of pity, like he was a dog about to be put to sleep, and then disappeared down the hall.

Matt ate away at the ice chips. His body ached, a result of what the doctor would call atrophy. He wished his parents were here. Surely, he could call or have the nurse -

"Matt?"

It was the same nurse from before, Dina. He had learned her name through the various backs and forths they had that night. He had also learned that she graduated from Boston University in 1987 with a degree in writing but had a change of heart during her thesis in Iowa, decided to go back to school for nursing, and fell in love with the PICU during her rotation. To Matt, she was gorgeous. She had a beauty mark on her chin and looked just like Cindy Crawford. She wore these blue pajama looking things that Dina would explain were called scrubs.

BOYS, BROKEN

She entered the room and came to his bedside. Beside him was a book of crosswords, which Matt loved. But these ones were really difficult. After struggling with them for twenty or so minutes he gave up. "How are you doing?"

He looked up at her with eyes that said *How does it look like I'm doing? Where's my family? What's going on?*

But he spoke better.

"I'm ok. Where are my folks? Do they know I'm awake? You're gonna call them, right Dina?"

———

Matt's parents arrived that morning (he had awoken at 3:15 AM), by 6:30 they were at his bedside. Marcia was confined to a wheelchair due to her broken pelvis and lower spinal fractures. She kept bumping into the edges of things with her wheelchair which, in Matt's opinion, made sense. This, *all* of this, was new to them.

Donald Rode stroked his son's hair.

"Matt," he said. "Oh, Matty. We love you so much."

"Dad -"

"Shhh," Donald said, and the room grew uncomfortably quiet. There was the faint electrical hum of the equipment in the room, and he could notice that both parents had been crying. For a moment, Matt's mind began to wonder about his room back home, and knew that he would eventually return to a house full of unpacked boxes, a ghost's room, since both Matt and his mother were in the hospital, and Donald would only go home to sleep (when he wasn't at work or at the hospital). Marcia held her son's hand and gave it a strong squeeze.

"I'm so sorry," Marcia said. "I didn't know."

Matt could not remember what she meant; his memory still foggy. But he did begin to feel a rush of something that he could not control. For the first time since he was a little kid he wept.

Matt remained at the hospital for the next few weeks, which was fine by him. Now that he was awake, he could spend time with his mother. Also, Dr. Stanley, the orthopedist, had started Matt on a slow regimen of rehabilitation.

"Basically," he began during one of the family's weekly status meetings, "Matt will need to teach himself to walk all over again."

"What do you mean? Like a toddler?" Donald Rode asked. The physician looked up from his notes like he was looking up at a waiter who had interrupted a potentially juicy business deal, and said "Actually, that's a great analogy. Not as chaotic, Mr. Rode, but similar. He shouldn't be bumping into too many tables. And don't worry," he said. "We have a strong relationship with the Northern Rehab Institute right down the street."

"Wait, you're Mmoving him?" Donald said. "But why? Has his healing progressed that fast?"

"Not quite, but he is out of the weeds" the doctor said. "And, to be blunt, we need the bed."

"But his leg!" Donald managed. "My wife. *His mother*. What are we going to do?"

Dr. Stanley sighed and looked directly at both Donald and Marcia.

"The fracture was transverse, which by itself can take anywhere from six weeks to six months to fully heal. We had to use intramedullary nailing, basically a long metal rod through the marrow canal of his leg. With adequate rehab he should be able to make a full recovery. Outpatient rehab, Mr. Rode. I promise, as long as your son puts in the effort, he will be able to walk again. There may be side effects, of course."

Marcia squeezed her son's hand.

"What do you mean?" Matt said. "Dr. Stanley, what kind of side effects?"

"The placement of the fracture, the location. I'll speak in layman's terms, Matt. It's near the part of your hip that your leg fits into." He took his fist and cupped it into his hand for emphasis. "You may have a limp on that side. You may never be able to run again. Some people say that they can feel it when they swim in especially cold waters. We don't know if or what you will experience, really, until we get you started."

A silence crept over the room, the reality sinking into Matt's eyes. Baseball? Skateboarding? No more? For a moment he looked as if to erupt, to scream. After a moment of silence, Matt said in a whisper, "And when can we start?"

Dr. Stanley looked at the family's faces, and then back to his notes.

"Normally," he began, "within 24 to 48 hours of the incident." The air felt like it was sucked out of the room, a pin drop being heard in an echo chamber with multiple plates. Matt thought, *I've been here for weeks. Weeks, damnit!* "But given that Matt had been unconscious all this time -"

"No, I'm ready," Matt said. "Today, let's sign me up. Let's do this. I'm ready." He looked at his father, his mother, eyes pleading yet hopeful. They nodded.

Dr. Stanley smirked. "Okay."

Rehab therapy was a bore at first, and Dr. Stanley had not lied. This was just like being a toddler again - he assumed; most days Matt couldn't remember what he had eaten for breakfast, let alone what it was like to evolve into a walking-talking-toddler-boy. He would use a walker, and the therapist would time him as he walked ten yards, the distance being marked on the ground with a piece of black masking tape. If he could make it to the tape and back in under twenty seconds, that was considered average for his condition. The first day he tried he scored forty-two. After a few weeks, he was down to thirteen. Once he was on crutches, he could make it in nine. Progress, slow and sure.

His parents would try to attend when they could, but with the accident, Don was working even more hours just to keep up with the new expenses of a wheelchair and other medical bills. The helicopter flight was just shy of six thousand dollars for each of them. When he had called his HMO to argue against the charges, the customer service representative had merely stated that the helicopter team was considered out-of-network, and therefore, denied. And when Donald Rode asked the representative how one goes about comparison shopping medi-flights while his wife and son are dying on an interstate highway, he was finally able to negotiate the costs down to three-grand a piece.

Matt graduated to the stairs, then strength training, and eventually by the middle of November, was able to help set the dinner table for Thanksgiving.

―――

It was a cold and bright day in February when Chucky didn't show up. The windchill was sixteen degrees and all the mothers had warned their children to *wear your scarves*. It was so cold that the snow banks, long ago frozen, had seemed almost willing to burst. Matt got to stay home from school on days like this. Hell, he got to stay home for most of the winter, but that was okay. He had a doctor's note stating he couldn't commute, especially if it was snowy (God forbid he fall and break his leg *again*), which was good. Who wants to go out in a New England February on purpose? It was also good because it was a guarantee he would get to see Chucky. He was given the sole responsibility of bringing Matt his homework and lessons every day, which meant they would really spend the afternoon eating Ellio's Pizza, drinking hot chocolate, and playing *Streets of Rage 2* - the best in the series, as far as they were concerned.

BOYS, BROKEN

Normally since the school day got out at 3:00 PM and Matt only lived a few blocks down the hill, Chucky would arrive at Matt's by 3:15 or 3:20 at the latest. Chucky's mother, Linda Dawson, would have called Marcia Rode if Chucky was sick and unable to make it. But that didn't happen. And as kids are wont to do, Matt just decided to make one less cup of cocoa in the microwave and start a one-player campaign (he chose Blaze, because she was *so hot*), and was at the elevator stage in Level 4, where he'd been busy fighting fat guys in a baseball field and the pitcher's mound all of a sudden drops from below like an elevator leading to an underground pit-fighting ring, when the doorbell rang. Matt, being spryer than his mother who was still adjusting to navigating the kitchen in a wheelchair, answered the door, his bad leg dragging behind in a series of limps.

"Is Chucky here?"

It was Cat.

"Cat, no," Matt said. "I figured he was at your house?"

"No, he's not, and he hasn't been home yet, and it's almost supper and"

"Is that Catherine?" Marcia called from the kitchen. She had been working on unrolling lasagna noodles but was struggling. The house was made in the early twentieth century and wasn't up to code for handicap access. "Does she want to stay for supper?"

"Can't, Mrs. Rode," she answered. "I was just seeing if my brother was here."

"Not here?" she asked. "But Matt, I thought I heard you two playing video games?"

"No, ma. Just me."

Cat rocked from one foot to the other, desperately trying to stay warm.

"Jesus, Matty, why haven't you invited her in? It's freezing outside!"

"It's o-o-kay, Mrs. R." Cat said. "I'm gonna try the twins. See if he's over-"

"Nah," Matt said. "They both got hockey practice over in Reading. Chucky wouldn't be there."
He paused.
"Come on. I think I know where he is."

Matt was better on the ice than the school, his doctor, or parents gave him credit for. It took some arm twisting, but Marcia finally agreed to let Matt join the search as long as he was home before supper hit the table, which by her account was forty-five minutes. He was also to find a ride if he was in trouble.

They had made it to the Olde Towne Memorial Library, a massive Greek revival decorated with columns and sharp-angled steps, reminiscent of the Capitol steps, only a few hundred miles away. The library normally closed at 8:30 on weeknights. When they stepped in, they were immediately greeted with a burst of warm air from the heating ducts that was welcoming, but quickly fogged Cat's glasses. They hung up their coats and made their way to the basement steps, noticing the *click-click-click* echo their footsteps made in the enormous vaulted ceiling. Down a double-set of staircases (Matt being extra careful to grab the wrought iron arm rail with both hands), and back to the brightly lit, semi-quiet Children's section, which was usually run by a mean-spirited, child hating old lady named Miss Duffy (the kids all called her Duff the Tough), but they didn't see her around.

Chucky was seated at a small table that was colored in bright primary splotches. He was bent over a pile of flashcards that, to a young man in college would appear very scholarly, but to a twelve-year-old just seemed very sad. Cat snuck up behind him and flicked him in his ear.

"Chuck!" she whisper-yelled. "Why didn't you call? Mom is pissed!"

"Oh shit," he said, normal volume. Wendy Appleton, the college education major doing her pre-practicum, chuckled from behind her desk.

"Keep it down, guys," she said to the kids. "And please...*language*." That last part came out in a way that immediately turned a gorgeous twenty-two-year-old into someone more in the ballpark of infinity.

"Sorry," Chucky said back.

"It's okay, but if Miss Duffy were here..." Wendy went back to her circulation.

Matt looks back at his friend.

"What gives, Chucky. I thought you were coming by?"

"Aronson, man. That's what gives."

At Reedy Pond Elementary, there were two choices for fourth grade - George Sharpe, and Leslie Aronson. Both were nice, both were distinguished, and like many suburban teachers in the early nineties, were both hell-bent on "making a difference." The difference between the two was teaching style and homework. Leslie Aronson routinely assigned stacks of worksheets and was known to surprise the class with spelling quizzes or vocab tests on words the kids knew they hadn't learned yet. Rumors flew that Mr. Sharpe would assign little to no reading or worksheets, instead regaling the class with anecdotes about actual life experiences. Imagine that. A mid-thirties teacher not using rote.

Everyone in the Gang managed to get Aronson.

"And now" Chucky said, "I'm stuck here doing flashcards 'cause she said there was the possibility, that we might-maybe-could have a quiz tomorrow-Friday-next week. That's the - she didn't say when! So, I'm a mess. You guys are looking at a mess. I mean, look at this one. 'Ironic.' The hell does that mean? Like it's made of iron?"

Cat asked Wendy to call her parents. After twenty minutes, they were picked up. Matt was in the door and washing his hands just as the lasagna made it to the table.

Chapter Four

By springtime, Matt had been back to school for a month-and-a-half, save for one early March storm that added another three inches to the frozen snowbanks. Marcia thought it best that Matt - who had given up the crutches just after Thanksgiving - would do best to sit that one out. The boy would have a limp for the rest of his life; there was simply no reason to add another wheelchair to the house. Times when he would jump into especially cold waters at Good Harbor beach would be enough to send aches up his side. But he didn't know that then.

Spring for Matt had always meant one thing - baseball. There was simply nothing better than to dust off his glove, lace up his cleats and hustle in the clay. He hit lefty but threw righty, a habit picked up by inheriting his father's glove, a beat-up relic if he had ever seen one. None of the other guys played little league, except for Eddie, but he spent the majority of his time playing for the Angels in left-center looking down at his feet as much as he looked up for the ball. Matt played shortstop, which was a tough position to play *without* a bum leg. Nearly every game saw him diving for wide hits or trying to avoid fast grounders he couldn't glove. He was a decent player, average hitter. Doug Moriarty, the Angels' coach, hadn't benched him yet, so that seemed promising.

He was better at the plate, a real Wade Boggs. He wasn't the power hitter of the Cansecos or McGwires, but on the frequent occasion he connected, he would usually be halfway to second before deciding if he should take the single. Now that he wasn't nearly as fast as he used to be, more often than not he would stay at first, and that was fine for Matt.

Practices were Monday and Wednesday from 4:00-7:00. Games were Tuesday and Thursdays at 6:00, or every other Saturday at 1:15. On the chance that Chucky, Cat, and Tommy would come to cheer on the Angels, it was usually on a Saturday. This always made Matt feel at home because they could have been doing dozens of other activities. Cat and Chucky had a circus-style trampoline and inground pool.

It was on one of these fateful Saturday games when the Gang first met the Sox, and nothing would ever be the same.

"Swing and a miss," the ump called. The Angels had been playing the White Sox, the hands-down best little league team in the county who also had arguably the best pitcher in the state, twelve-year-old Danny Johnson. The league ranged from third grade through sixth. Danny was on the older side and due to his prowess and strength not afforded to prepubescent boys; he merely had to think of throwing his fastball inside to make the younger kids piss themselves. League rules were that everyone including pitcher do "at bats," so Danny was in the cage warming up, swinging back and forth gently as to not disturb his pitching arm. Eric Mazzola, a skinny frog of a boy who sat in front of Matt in homeroom, was up at bat. Count was two-and-two.

Max Roger, the Angels' pitcher who was, like Matt, a decent player, wound up and threw, the ball sailing, closer closer -

Eric bunted. This caught Matt off guard who, by reflex would guard the mound, but Max hadn't moved. Chaos ensued. Sean Tully, the Angels' catcher, tossed off his mask, found the ball trailing up the third base line and gunned it towards first. Eric, who would have been safe at first, saw what Sean and Johnny, the first baseman, hadn't - the throw was wild. But by the time Johnny got the ball and tried to calculate the situation, Eric had passed Matt and was safe at third.

"What the ever-loving shit was that!?" Coach Moriarty yelled, throwing his paper cup of Gatorade. "Come on! Hustle! What. I can't - You guys know the plays! We've been over this a thousand times!" He was kicking dirt at the bench.

The players returned to their positions. Next up was Danny Johnson, who wasn't known as a great hitter, always protecting that throwing arm. But they had a man on third.

"Come on, son!" came a shout from the bleachers. Matt didn't have to look to see that it was Danny's father, Kevin Johnson. Kevin, a fifteen-year career patrolman in Reedy Pond, was easily identified by his uniform blues.

Max wound up -

Another bunt.

"Son of a-" came out of Moriarty's mouth, but Sean had caught the bounce. He threw to first for the out, and Johnny threw it back to home. Eric Mazzola had a step on Sean, but he made the tag in the end. Sean was due up after the inning change, followed by Max and Matt - and need be, Eddie. But that was when the massacre began.

"Good job, guys" Moriarty said. "Good hustle. Really turning it around." He took a sip of his red Gatorade. "Sean, nice arm."

Matt looked at Sean.

"What do you think?"

"About?"

"Think they have a plan?" Matt asked.

"Yeah," Eddie said. "Make sure we leave with less teeth than we came here with."

He chuckled. No one else did.

BOYS, BROKEN

Sean got a solid double, Max struck out. Now Matt was up at the plate, tapping the clay from his cleats with the end of his bat though there wasn't any stuck to begin with.

"Batter up," the ump called. "One down."

Before he even looked up, he heard -

"Strike one!"

What, he thought. *Couldn't be that fast.* He heard a snicker from beneath him, or was it behind him?

"Gonna get you, new kid. Been waiting all year," Corey Whitaker, the White Sox catcher said. Matt could have sworn he heard him mumble something that sounded like "fuck-stick," and became terrified. This guy, a behemoth of a sixth grader was known to throw fully-clothed kids into the MDC pool down the road. Matt swore he was six feet tall. He had 26 home runs that season. In kid's ball.

Corey threw the ball back to Danny.

Matt leaned in and this time could feel the air as it breezed by his cheek.

"Ball," Ump said.

Count was one and one.

"C'mon Matty!" he heard from the bleachers. Matt looked up and wasn't surprised to see it was Cat, sitting with Chucky and Tommy, who was eating an enormous pink cotton-candy.

"You got this, Matt!" Chucky agreed.

"Strike two!" the ump disagreed.

Count was one and two, no risk playing it safe. He would swing at whatever came next. *Swing away and he won't even expect it, yeah. I'll show Danny and Corey and all of them what the New Kid can do*, Matt thought. And that was when the pitch was thrown, and it was a beauty - it was as if time had slowed down, and if he looked just right he could count the stitches sailing through the air as if guided by unknown, invisible strings tethered to Matt's bat. This was the one - The Pitch To End All Pitches. He stepped into it and -

CRACK!

The bat connected and Matt took off, his legs pounding clay, his arms buzz sawing against his sides, his leg throbbing as it quietly pip-pip-pipped in and out of the socket. He didn't look up as he was rounding first when he began to hear the shouts.

"Oh shit," Chucky cried from the bleachers.

Commotion. Noise from both sides of the diamond.

"What? What happened?" Cat asked.

Tommy had risen to his feet pointing at the pitcher's mound where a newly doubled-over, screaming Danny Johnson lay piled like a mess of coats in the spare bedroom at a holiday party. It appeared he was cupping his crotch.

"That's what," he said. "Methinks *our* boy just screwed over *their* boy."

Back on the diamond was chaos. Most of the Sox had crowded the mound, Coach Hughes was kneeling next to Danny. Both the ump and Coach Moriarty also arrived, moved the teammates away, *give the boy some room* they hollered. Sean looked at Matt from across third base, where he was still positioned. *Technically*, he thought to himself, *the ball is still in play. I think Sean could legally score.*

"What do we do," Sean mouthed to Matt, who answered with a faceless shrug. For the time being, he was going to stay the hell put. Danny had now shifted so he was on his back staring at the sky. It was strangely quiet, the way it feels in-between gusts of wind. The silence then turned into a weird, groan-moan which transitioned into a coughing/retching-moan, and Matt realized then that he had been too preoccupied running to first to notice he had smashed a line drive directly at -

"My fucking balls!" Danny Johnson screamed.

There were audible gasps from the crowd, some snickers from some kids skateboarding nearby. The conversation between the ump and the coaches was becoming heated and Matt knew immediately that they were calling the game, calling it because of the damn New Kid, and now Moriarty was throwing his hat and shouting at the ump, and when he looked away, the first face Matt saw was Danny Johnson's, and then Corey Whitaker ("Hey, Fuck-stick") who, if asked later, would have sworn had grown six inches in the past five minutes, and when he looked back towards Sean and saw that he was already back at the dugout, panic struck because now Matt was all alone on the field with most of the Sox, including another monster named P. J. Armstrong and he did what any rational kid would do. He ran as fast as he could towards Chucky and his friends at the bleachers, and if he had ignored the *clop clop clop* sound of his cleats in the clay, he may have heard Corey warn "You're dead."

After baseball season had ended, the Gang spent most of their afternoons avoiding the Sox who clearly had it out for Matt, and by proxy, them. This was made infinitely easier due to a few facts. First, the older kids were in fifth and sixth grade, went to the beautifully acorn-strewn-and-misnamed-Elm Street Middle School, located all the way down the other end of Main Street and Pine Ave. Since Reedy Pond Elementary was only a few blocks from both Matt and Chucky it was easy to get to one of their houses before the big kids showed up. Second, everyone stuck together. This included Cat. Chucky didn't think that Danny or Whitaker would go after his sister, as young as she was, but she did have a mouth on her and was known to cuss at whoever was in her way. Chucky didn't want those people to be Johnson, Whitaker and the rest of the Sox.

Most of their time was spent playing the latest *Street Fighter* or *Mortal Kombat* - Eddie and Tommy had discovered the latter, a particularly gruesome beat-em-up at an arcade in New Hampshire called Fun Spot while vacationing at Weirs Beach. Matt and Chucky were okay players, but it was Cat who excelled in all matters of decapitations, electrocutions, and skeletal burnings. Of course, when they played these games, either on Matt's Sega or Chucky's SNES, they had to keep the volume turned low, or else their doting mothers would pry as often as mothers do. They wouldn't mute the television, though, because frankly, they enjoyed the splats and screams.

The days continued in routine until one day, Matt realized he was being handed his final report card and was being ushered out the door - after a final cleaning out of his locker, of course. The mid-June sun was spectacular on his face, and there was a slight sweetness to the air. He waited for Chucky and the twins like he always did, by the bike rack near the swings where he took his spectacular fall almost a year ago.

He opened his report card and wasn't surprised that he had passed, but not exceedingly well. He got a C-plus in Math, a C-plus in Science, and two B's (Social Studies and English). Gym was pass/fail, so he didn't bother factoring in the "P." Not terrible. Not particularly great, either. He wouldn't give this to his father after a long day on State Street and say "Gee, dad. Hang this on the fridge, would ya?" But it was good enough to graduate with his friends, which was what mattered most. Graduate with his friends and move on to the -

He gulped.

To the Middle school, he thought, where the Big Kids were. We won't be able to hide out when *they* are right there, and *we* are a mile-and-a-half away from home. His panic turned to terror. What would happen, say, if Johnson were to get some of his buddies and play "Let's Chase the Gimp?" He couldn't outrun them. They were bigger, faster, stronger. And even if Chucky and the twins were with him, it wouldn't matter. The Sox could take them all on, even if The Gang did know all the combos in *Mortal Kombat*. He ruminated on this, and his breathing increased. Heart racing. Palms clammy. Chest tense.

"Hey!"

He died, for a split second he was dead and in the ground near these swings and that was that. Or he was in the car during the accident, mangled and bleeding for not wearing a seatbelt, or he never really woke up from that coma, did he? That's it. That's it.

It was Cat.

"Jesus Christ, don't do that to me!"

"Sorry," she said. Who pissed in your Froot Loops?"

Normally, a remark like this would have brought him to the point of absolute giggles. But not now. Not now.

"How'd you do?" Matt said, collecting himself. He didn't really remember what kind of metric the third grade used to rank aptitude but thought that if she was curious about his grades, it was the least he could ask.

"Great!" she exclaimed, all smiles, the afternoon sun shining miles through her hair. "I know it's gonna be a great summer. I can just tell."

Chapter Five

Reedy Pond had two sets of train tracks. One was an old freight line that bisected Main Street and passed through town on rusted tracks overgrown with weeds. Twice a year during spring and fall, a forty-car behemoth slowly crept its way through town to Miller Stone Works where the cabs would be filled with tons and tons of powdered stone dust and concrete. From there, the train would head to more northern points like Portsmouth, Bangor, Augusta. From there it would turn and commence its trek south towards more hospitable climes. The other set of tracks came from Boston, and hugged the marsh near the lake, aiming towards Haverhill and New Hampshire. This was a commuter rail. On its journey through town, it cut through the Westside neighborhood, traveling under a decrepit expanse known as the Tyler Street bridge, an old condemned structure that spanned over the tracks thirty feet below, and across to Ruddles Avenue where it would meet with Center Street. At one point, long before any of the Gang were alive, you could drive across the bridge because, well, that's what it was meant for. It was a narrow bridge, so much so, that only one car could pass at any given time in either direction. And though Tyler Street wasn't the busiest section in town, it would still cause quite a backup during rush hour traffic, as it was one of the only ways to bypass the red lights at the rail crossings around town.

BOYS, BROKEN

At one point in time, it was brought to a vote in a Council meeting to widen the bridge. This was way before Matt was born. The town's Board of Selectman didn't think it was an appropriate use of funds and earmarked other priorities instead. After the first couple of bad New England winters with no plowing or sanding, the pavement started to blister.

A few years later the joists would begin to erode. The town decided to shut down the bridge to all car traffic after state inspectors from the Department of Transportation deemed the structure "in disrepair." Pedestrian foot-traffic was still allowed, however. The bridge was, after all, the most convenient way to get from the West side of town, over the tracks, and to the lake without having to sit in traffic at the crossing on Walter Hill. It wasn't until some years before Matt Rode arrived in Reedy Pond that pedestrian traffic on the bridge would also cease to exist.

The story was that one Halloween, some teenage boys from the nearby town of Reading had parked at the foot of the bridge with the express and sole purpose of getting ripped and pissing into the fans on the roof of an oncoming train bound for God Knows Where. One of the boys, Dave Pelham was weary of the idea that his friend, sixteen-year-old Mark Glosser, had come up with while being absolutely piss-drunk on his stepfather's Cutty Sark, but Dave decided to go along and see the deed through, anyway. What can you say? The decisions we make as kids, right?

"This whole world, man," Mark had said. "This is all just piss. We're dust and ants and shit. Traveling from one place to the next." Young Master Glosser didn't realize just how correct he was to being "dust and ants and shit," or what was about to happen when he went out that night, but he was certainly more excited than his friend.

The lamplight of the train drew closer in the distance and a shaky Mark Glosser grasped the railing with both hands.

"Help me up, dickweed," he said to Dave, who gave him a ten-finger boost. The duo stood on the handrails, thick wooden railroad ties that were joined together by long, firm bolts. They stood, waited for a rumbling sound, and when they saw the train come, and the boys whipped out *their* bolts, the railing that had once supported them gave way. It didn't break in half, but the center bolt cut through the wooden tie, old and rotted and infested with termites - the sudden jolt gave the railing a shake and both boys tumbled the thirty or so feet head first onto the train tracks. From that day on, a chain link fence was erected on both entrances of the bridge with "Condemned" and "Danger - No Trespassing By Order of the Police" signs.

This, of course, was where the Gang was headed to on their first official day of summer.

———

You could see the bridge from the twins' backyard which spanned about half an acre of blackberry bushes and tall grass before turning into a wiry thicket of brambles and deadwood. By late June or early July you could sprint your way down; in the early spring or late fall, however, it was always best to attempt any hiking to the bridge slowly, as the thicket was apt to turn gooshy out of nowhere and eat your shoes and socks.

"C'mon, guys!" Nickie shouted. "Wait up! I don't know where we're going!" She was trailing behind the boys by about thirty feet. Cat stayed by her friend's side, although she knew this route like the back of her hand. The boys continued deeper into the brush, as the grasses and brambles grew taller and thornier. Their mothers knew that it was not uncommon for their kids to go out in the morning to play and come home in evenings bleeding all over from the scratches and pricks of time-forgotten nature.

After twenty yards or so the mud would turn into a sudden and steep embankment comprised of a similar clay found in baseball fields. Once down the slope, you were less than ten feet from the southbound tracks, so it was of the utmost importance to be aware and pay attention to the time. Normally, they would confine any time

BOYS, BROKEN

for exploring out here to strictly early afternoon/pre-rush hour times, when there weren't as many chances to get caught or - worse - killed. Commuter trains didn't need to announce their arrival coming around the bend in a deserted area miles from the actual crossing. But in the rare instances a conductor would see some vagrant child on the tracks, you could believe that horn would blow.

It was a hell of a lot easier going down the embankment than trying to climb up it, so when it was time to leave, the boys and girls would walk along the tracks, southbound towards town, darting into the woods whenever a train came, until they reached Mrs. Harrington's house. Lydia Harrington, an ex-substitute teacher at Reedy Pond Memorial High School ("Go Tigers!"), could usually be found in her Laz-E-Boy eating soup and watching soaps, as rumor had it. Most of her hearing had gone, and since Medicare wouldn't cover hearing aids, most of the time she would have Bob Barker or the *Press Your Luck* guy on at full-tilt. This was good for the Gang, since she would never notice when they snuck through her yard and out onto Elm and Walnut. They were about to turn onto Elm when Matt felt something whiz by his head.

"Hey, *asshole*!"

Without turning, Matt knew it was Corey Whitaker, which was bad, and that he was throwing rocks, which was worse. His suspicions were confirmed when he heard that voice again. "Pukeface, I'm talking to you!"

They all turned, and that's when he realized he was right, though he wished he wasn't. It wasn't *just* Corey. Danny Johnson was with him, as well as brothers Jason and Jackson Hill, and another monster of a kid by the name of Tony Quinn. The girls shrieked. Jason Hill was holding what appeared to be a dead squirrel by the tail, though it wasn't roadkill, which was somehow more terrifying. Jason was known to be quite a whittler in Cub Scouts.

"Hey," Eddie shouted. "What do you want with us? We didn't do anything to you guys."

"You know," began Corey, and spat on the ground. "You're right. *You* didn't do shit. Hell, the only thing you and your double are good at is choking your hoses. But *him*-" He pointed at Matt. "That gimp cost us our perfect season. Cost Danny his right nut."

At any other time, a remark like this would have caused the boys to erupt in laughter, but this was not one of those times. Corey continued.

"I figured we'd let Danny return the favor."

"What do you mean?" Chucky asked but had a feeling he knew the answer already. He side-eyed Matt and realized that *he* knew it more. For some reason, Matt inched closer to Corey, pleading.

"It was an accident!" Matt yelped. He could feel his heart beating faster, palms starting to sweat. Even when surrounded by his cluster of friends, he was utterly lost in panic. "Come on, Corey. You don't really want this."

Looking into that monster's eyes, Matt could tell there was no room to negotiate.

"*He* doesn't want shit."

It was Danny's voice, coming from behind.

"But *I* want to kick your ass, Matt." The Sox began their march towards their prey, enveloping around the kids in a motley circle like you would find in a dance club, except in this case no one was cabbage-patching into the middle. It was now just two contenders, Danny and Matt. There is no bell. In street fights, there never is. Just the constant noise of chattering henchmen from both teams.

"Look, Danny, I'm really sorry you got hurt. It was a-"

"An accident," Chucky said.

"An accident," Matt echoed. "But it's over. It's all over we don't want any trouble -"

The cacophony turns into static, a pink background that hangs like clouds. Matt quickly scans his opponent up and down and thinks *Okay, I do not have size on my side, neither strength nor speed - if I go for the face with a jab, even connecting hard, he's going to hook me with his right - his pitching hand - and that would put me down quickly - if I go for a hook, I'd be swinging up - he'd dodge -*

Matt was punched in the face.

The fist, which appeared out of nowhere, connected with his left cheek. Matt could feel it down in his legs, the flesh began to swell and knew it would bruise. He cried out in a mix of pain and fear, tried to swing and wasn't surprised that he missed. Danny countered with a quick one-two that sent Matt stumbling back on his heels, arms reeling. Television and movies never really show how it feels to be punched in the face. Matt wasn't prepared for how quick and effortless it was until it had happened the first time, and now that it had happened again, he didn't have the time to react to the next punch, or the next after, this one a suckerpunch coming from Corey Whitaker up into his solar plexus, emptying his wind and dropping Matt to the ground with a whimpering thud. He knew he was going to puke.

"You asshole!" Chucky screamed, charging straight for Whitaker. He attempted to tackle him, and managed to knock each other over, Whitaker onto his back. But Chucky, much like the dog who didn't know what to do with the car he just caught, froze for a split second - enough time for the Hill brothers to grab him up and hurl Chucky off into the gravel. Matt got hit three more times before Eddie and Tommy rushed in.

It was bedlam. Nicki had run off crying. Cat screamed.

"Stop it!" Lydia Harrington barked. "Stop it this instant!" She had come out onto her porch. Through the open door, Matt could still hear the *Family Feud* host asking the contestants to "Name Something You'd Always Keep On Hand In Case Of An Emergency," and he screamed *"A ROCKETSHIP"* before finally emptying his stomach.

Chucky got back up and looked ready to swing if coerced, but that didn't matter. They weren't here for Chucky. They were here for Matt, and they had got him. By the time Tommy and Chucky were helping Matt up off the ground, the Sox were gone, halfway down the block and hollering all the way. All in all, the first day of summer had started out okay, Matt had thought, and hopefully now that Danny had gotten this stupid fight out of his system, maybe the rest of the summer will be great, right?

If asked later, he wouldn't be able to tell if he was being sarcastic or not.

The curtain of the hospital room swung open and Allie Rode appeared, like she was part of the finale on a David Copperfield magic special. What she saw didn't make any sense. Here was her husband, sitting on a hospital bed dressed in textured socks and scrubs. Today was Thursday. She knew, even though she was never awake to see him leave in the morning - goddamn who leaves for their shift at four in the AM - she knew that Thursday was Cornflower Blue Dress Shirt And Chinos Day, not hospital scrubs. No, none of this made any sense at all.

"Matt, sweety. Matt. Sweety. What the hell is going on?"

Matt looked up at his wife through red, puffy eyes. She couldn't tell if they were from crying or lack of sleep; by this point, neither would have surprised her.

She came to him and sat, wrapped her arms around him in a sideways hug. They were silent for a long time.

"Matt," she said, finally. "Matt, listen. The security guard said they won't let you leave. Do you get that?"

He nodded twice.

"I know, but -"

"What are we going to do?" she asked. "If you are stuck here? Isn't there anyone we can call? Someone you know at the hospital? I mean, this is a huge deal, Matt. This isn't some...some-" She snapped her fingers at Jerry to get his attention "- some bureaucratic bullshit that you can just shrug off, right?"

"Correct, Ma'am," Jerry responded.

"Matt, this is serious, serious shit," she continued, eyes back to her husband. "Legal. You can't just fucking leave because you're having a bad day. Or that you're sad. Or that - "

"I know! I know!" Matt shouted, taking Jerry by surprise. Up until this point he figured the quiet guy in Bay 3 was just that, like a field mouse, not wanting to bother anyone. The last thing he needed was to put somebody in restraints. God, he hated putting skinny guys in restraints. You'd think it'd be so easy, but they're all wiry.

"Mr. Rode let's be..." he started, but Matt continued.

"I know what this is. I know all about being Sectioned. I can't leave because they think I may be a threat. And you want to know why? Because I am, I fucking am!"

"Matty," she said, tears on her cheeks.

"Do you know what I was doing this morning, Al. What I've been doing every morning? Or why I leave so goddamn early everyday? Before my shift?"

"No, hon," she said.

None of this feels good.

Matt paused like he was thinking of each exact word he was about to say next, like trying to solve a puzzle. "Across the street from work is the parking garage for the hospital. About six, seven stories. Not counting the roof. There's one guy at the gate who does overnights. Carl. And I know Carl, and he knows me. Cause every single morning I walk past him dressed for work as I take the elevator to the top floor, which is the roof. See, you can park on the roof, not sure if I said that. Every morning I go up there, I take a look over the Charles, stand on the ledge and think 'Is it high enough?' Just like that. *Every day* I do this," he says. His head twitches.

Gonna get you, fuckstick.

His hands go to his temples and rubs.

"The past couple of weeks, though. Different places, different garages. WHAT'S IT GONNA TAKE?"

By this time Matt looks up and realizes he's begun shouting, notices his wife is openly crying, and Jerry has taken out his walkie. He holds up his hand to say "Hold on." Again, he combs his hand through his hair, squints very hard, and wishes he'd had some coffee.

"But tonight," he mutters. "This morning - whenever, was different."

Allie goes to him.

"You stopped yourself? Had second thoughts?"

Matt shook his head at her.

"Got caught this time."

"Matt!" And now it's her voice that has risen. "What about Gabe? Me? Son-of-a-bitch, you can't just – I mean, what were you thinking?"

"The easiest part about making a decision like this, honey," he begins. "Is having to rationalize it."

It was late August, a few weeks since the anniversary of Matt's big accident the previous year. For the most part, Matt and the Gang had managed to avoid the Sox and in particular, Johnson and Whitaker. There was the one time, however, that Matt had broken their rule about sticking together. He was down the street at the House of Pizza waiting on an order for his folks.

He asked Niko how long it would be and decided to kill some time feeding quarters into the latest Mortal Kombat machine. House of Pizza had a small game room with a stellar selection of choices, limited normally to the latest and greatest. Matt had no idea how they made their choices, but one day you were playing Street Fighter II, and the next weekend, the Turbo Edition arrived. There was also a mint edition of Addams Family pinball that Matt adored. But at this particular time, he was determined to figure out the new fatalities in Mortal Kombat II if it killed him. And in this case, he might later think, maybe it almost did.

BOYS, BROKEN

It was round two of his third run at a new character, Baraka. Matt, who was always Sub-Zero, had mastered the art of freezing his opponent with an ice ball, and then doing a deep jump kick/uppercut combo. If timed right, Baraka would be dead meat in a few goes. But, like most things he would soon realize, Matt was having shit luck. The CPU was kicking his ass; every time he tried to jump kick, Baraka would counter with a scissor attack with his forearm blades. He kept at it, but no dice. Pretty soon, he heard the announcer say FINISH HIM, and then Matt watched as his character was sent flying into a pool of acid by a wicked uppercut. After a few seconds, the bare-boned skeleton floated to the surface. The word FATALITY appeared on the screen dripping with blood. *Sure got that right*, he thought.

"Order's up!" Niko said in his thick Greek accent. "Ketchup, salt, pepper?"

"Nah, I'm good," Matt said and handed him a twenty. Niko counted out the change and handed it back to Matt. "You the boy play baseball, in the accident? Last summer?"

"Yes, I am," Matt said, grabbing the pizza and wondering why his accident had any place in the life of a pizza store owner. "My name's Matt."

"Well, you know, Matt" Niko replied. "You seem a good one. You come here, day after day I see you. You spend your quarters on these games, and for what?"

"They're fun," he smiled. "Gotta chase that high score."

"They rot your brain," Niko said. "Kid spends all his money in damned machines. Rots your brain. Chase scores? Should be chasing girls or ground balls. Tragedy, I say. But fuck do I know, right?"

He smiled as the kid walked out the door. To a mostly empty shop Niko says, "Boy his age. Wastes their youth. No ideas, but eh-"

The phone rang twice, and Niko picked it up. "Delivery or pickup?"

Since he was no good at even attempting to balance something on his handlebars Matt had walked to House of Pizza, even though it was a little far, but he didn't mind in the slightest. The smell of the pizza was intoxicating. Surprisingly, it was not muggy at this time in the evening, and it would give the pizza just enough time to "settle," as his mother would say. The worst part about fresh pizza is grabbing a slice only to have the majority of the cheese fall off like the Three Stooges doing one of their yanking-at-the-table-cloth gags.

He made it from Auburn Avenue to Main Street and walked over the train tracks at the depot and headed towards Perry Way. There, just outside the All-NITE Variety Store was Danny Johnson. He appeared to be alone, but that was when Corey Whitaker appeared with a fountain soda in his hand. Neither of the boys had a bike, which, Matt figured, was because Danny lived on Cedar Court a few blocks away. Matt felt the same way - nice night, why let it go to waste?

He decided that the best approach to avoid them was to wait to see if they were going in a different direction then he was or be tip-toe quiet and keep his distance until they turned off. He began to follow, and as he did, he could hear parts of the boys' conversation. Whitaker had said something about "Finding a bunch of rubbers at the cemetery by the lake. If you look inside 'em, you can see the sperms." Danny Johnson did not believe the facts of this particular anecdote at all. *His* brother, he said, had *done it,* with *six* girls already, and none of them ever met any sperms - his sousaphone playing brother was also the ripe age of seventeen and didn't get many date requests on Friday nights. Their conversation stayed more or less on this path, and Matty had kept his distance, a good twenty yards behind. The discussion soon turned into classic "Yo Momma" jokes (Yo Momma so fat she got baptized at Seaworld), and then it hit him: Danny and Corey were kids, just like him. All they wanted to do was get into just the kind of trouble Matt's friends wanted. He was certain that given the opportunity, those guys were good, decent people. This was their summer, too. They were just enjoying the cool night breeze as much as he was. And maybe it was unfair of him to be so negative all the time, judging these kids without really knowing them.

And that was when Matt tripped on his shoelace, and all those preconceived notions came back hard.

"Of course, I love you," Matt said to an Allison Rode he had not seen in a long time. Of course, he *had* seen her, just this morning as he left the bedroom at 2:30 AM, in fact. But the one he was looking at now, those eyes. This was alien. She was full of fear, full of hurt. And he wanted to weep. He let out a breath like he had been wincing. "You two, only you, are my everything."

"But why?" she asked. "I don't- I'm sorry, I just don't understand. I guess, I don't get it." She took a puff on her inhaler that she had pulled from her purse. "Sorry. I just-"

"Sit down," Matt said. "Sweety, sit down. Don't have an attack over this."

She paused, but she didn't sit.

"Why?" she asked.

"Why? Because you need to breathe, Al." And now she was across the room, her back turned to him. When she turned back, he could see streaks in her mascara.

"No. Why now? Why do this to us?" she asked. "Is it me, Matt? Or what? Tell me. Have I failed you as a wife?" Her eyes were more hurt than concerned. Actually, she looked damn pissed. "Don't you think I get sad, too?" Her words hit him like a slap he didn't feel he totally deserved.

"That's bullshit. That's not *fair*. I'm *not* sad," Matt shouted. His hands flailed in his lap with nowhere to go. "I'm not sad and I'm *not* crazy! Stop looking at me like I woke up today fully conscious of planning to ruin your life. I'm sorry you missed your closing. I'm sorry I can't pick up Gabe tonight. I'm sorry! But I'm your husband, goddamnit. And I can't believe you wouldn't get how much it hurts me that you seem to be siding with -" His voiced dropped to a whisper. "- with them."

"Well, boo fucking hoo," Allie said. Fresh tears appeared on her cheeks.

Matt stood. Normally at this point in the argument when the insults started and the nervous adrenaline kicked in, his only option was to flee the scene, to go anywhere but here. But there was nowhere to go. Nowhere unless he wanted to get clothes-lined by Sailor Jerry over there, Matt thought, and that almost made him grin. He sat back down.

There was a long silence that seemed to have stretched for hours. Allie's cellphone rang - actually vibrated this time - and she answered.

"Hi, Ma," she spoke, and Matt felt nausea rise in his throat. "Yup, thanks for picking him up." There was a pause. "Not sure. No one's been in since - hon, when did they take your blood?"

"Eleven thirty."

"Eleven thirty, ma," she continued. She covered the receiver with her hand and whisper-screamed at Matt. *"Four hours? Are you fucking* -, uh yeah, ma? No idea. He would love mac and cheese." Another pause. "Sure, give him a bath if he wants one."

She hung up the phone, and the argument which had been interrupted, seemed to just fizzle. She walked over to her husband and sat down next to him, leaned her head on his shoulder.

"Cheryl?"

"Yeah," Allison said. "She picked him up. Will put him to bed if she has to."

"That's nice of her," he said taking her hand in his.

"Yeah," she answered, sounding very tired.

BOYS, BROKEN

Another fifteen minutes of silence pass when good friend Jerry enters the room, but this time he is not alone. A man is with him, Matt pegs him for late thirties given the hipster bowtie, though his sport coat and nicotine-stained fingers may suggest a bit older.

"Mr. Rode," the man says, his voice that of a gravelly professor. "My name is Dr. Cliven Baxter. I am the on-call psychiatrist on the unit today, and I do apologize tremendously for your wait." He looks down at the chart, makes a face like he sees something he doesn't like, flips a page over, then back to the cover sheet. "I'm sorry, I was finishing up with another patient." He glances behind him towards the hallway. Out of the corner of his mouth says, "This isn't your chart," to no one in particular. He pulls a stool over and continues without missing a beat. "But that's okay. I was reading over your file and was wondering if you wouldn't mind speaking in private."

"Isn't this…" Matt looked confused. "Aren't we speaking in private now, doctor?"

The doctor looked at Allie.

"Mrs. Rode?" he asked.

There was a brief pause. She looked as confused as Matt did. Confused and tired.

"Am I supposed to do something?" she said, her voice earnest as much as it was annoyed.

"Yes, Mrs. Rode. I'd like you to leave," he said in a cold tone that sounded like he harbored a legitimate grudge against strangers. "Mrs. Rode, I'd like to have a chat with Mr. Rode, and I can only discuss with Mr. Rode in private if you are not present, correct? HIPAA, Mrs Rode."

Allie stood up.

"Doctor, no offense, but whatever the hell you're about to ask my husband, I think I have the right to know."

"Hon," Matt says. "It's okay."

"The hell it is!" she cries, and that is when the tears come back.

"Mrs. Rode," Baxter begins.

"No, sir." Allie says. "We've been here all damn day. You've already reviewed his file, you said. And now you want to ask him more? But why would you need to ask him if you reviewed what he's told everyone else all day long? Nothing has changed! I want him to get help. He obviously wants help. Can't this just be-"

She stops. Besides Matt's shaking knee, there is an utter silence in the room, like the sound displaced after a vacuum tube is turned off.

"Allie," Matt whispers. "Come here." He takes her head in his hands, kisses her cheek, puffy with running blush. "Let me answer his questions, and then we'll see what they have to say. We'll make a plan."

"But, babe -"

"And if they need to do more testing, or whatever, we'll put our feet down then, right? We'll say go screw, and go home and see Gabe and get pad thai, right?"

"Yes, okay," she says, wiping her nose.

Allie picked up her purse and headed towards the door before turning around, walking towards Matt. "I didn't want to forget this," she said, picking up her cardigan draped over her seat. She walked out the door, her shadow fading with her footsteps as she disappeared down the hall.

"Doc, you can ask me whatever you want," Matt says. "Anything."

Corey and Danny heard a sound from behind them and when they turned, couldn't believe what they were looking at. The Gimp must have fallen into a bunch of trash cans or something, because he was on the ground and having a hell of a time.

"Lookie here," Danny said, and started to laugh. "What a fucking waste!"

BOYS, BROKEN

The two advanced towards Matt, who froze. His left leg was killing him, and he knew that even if he could make it to his feet, he couldn't outrun either of them. From his vantage point, the sidewalk extended into infinity, far past these two boys growing larger and larger. To an outside observer it would appear as if Matt had rolled onto his back and was trying some elaborate backwards crab-walk, and then Danny was on top of him, pinning his knees into Matt's collar bones, still weak from the jungle-gym accident, creating a terribly unpleasant restraint. Corey picked up the box of pizza from the ground and took out a slice.

"What's this? Extra cheese? Does it come with a side order of garlic NUTS?" he asked and kicked Matt in the groin before he had a chance to scream. Danny reached for the box, grabbing a slice and shoved it into Matt's face. Choking on pizza, throbbing from the nut-shot and being pinned down, Matt had nowhere to go. He imagined this was what drowning victims felt.

Summer's sun died into crumbling autumn leaves, and Tommy and Eddie moved away. And like with many kids of a certain age, promises to stay in touch were made, but promises were merely words. The Gang was cut down to three, and Matt and Chucky were starting at the Elm Street Middle School, leaving Cat alone across town. They lucked out in fifth grade for two reasons: Mr. Higgins and Billy Shaw. Mr. Higgins was their homeroom and social studies teacher, was a Reedy Pond townie, and knew Chucky's mother from back in the day.

"Me and your father used to go at it during school, over Linda - uh - your mother. You know, I took her to prom, but your dad got her hand in the end," he said one day in the hall, a little whimsical. "Funny how it all works out."

A few weeks later, Mr. Higgins had pulled Matt aside. *Fuck*, Matt thought. The previous Friday they were assigned to write an essay on "Where the Red Fern Grows," and Matt immediately thought he was going to get reamed. He had trouble coming up with an argument about the people in the book, which he didn't get at all, with the kids and their fighting. He wrote something about the ferns themselves, and the dogs, and death.

"Matt don't take this the wrong way," the teacher said. "Well, that came out wrong. You can take this any way you want. What I meant to ask was, did you have any help on this paper? From your parents, maybe?"

Oh no, Matt thought. He thinks I cheated.

"No sir," he began. "Mom's not much of a reader, and dad's more of a John Grisham man." Higgins went on to explain a lot of things Matt didn't understand about the fern, the dogs, and then said "Matt, do you know what symbolism is, son?"

Matt shook his head slowly.

"It doesn't mean you think I cheated, does it?"

"No," Higgins said. The paper received an A-minus and ended up on the refrigerator.

The second part of the autumn that was a good omen was the arrival of Billy Shaw. He moved to Reedy Pond from a small town in New Hampshire's White Mountains, relocating into the neighborhood where the twins used to live. This type of divine providence made it clear to both Matt and Chucky of one thing - they would automatically be friends with Billy Shaw. Though Matt and Chucky had stolen glances of him in the hallways at school and eating alone in the cafeteria, they didn't truly meet him until one early afternoon at the House of Pizza, mashing buttons on *Street Fighter II*.

At first glance, they had been intimidated. Billy stood nearly six feet tall and had to weigh at least a buck-twenty. He was a solid kid, but his deft fingers handled the joystick with a finesse that other mashers lacked. Matt had observed that Billy didn't spend a lot of time at home, going straight to the game room after school most days, even when there was no one else to play. Matt assumed that this could mean he was a loner, he didn't need a team, he was all set. But Matt also thought that his height and strength would certainly beef up their chances if they ever had another run-in with The Sox - they would always refer to anyone who hung around with Danny and Corey as The Sox, even though most of their baseball days were behind them - playing shortstop for the Angels was the last regulated league Matt Rode would ever play in. But there was something else about him - Matt was too young to know what word he would use to describe it. What was that the French said? He didn't know.

Chucky walked over to Billy and rested a quarter on the screen, the unspoken and universal sign of dibs.

"Next up," he said. Billy didn't look away from the screen. He was playing as Chun-Li and continued to beat the ever-loving piss out of Sagat, a shirtless and muscular fighter the game claimed hailed from Iran, deflecting every blow his opponent had thrown. Chun-Li's propeller-kick sent Sagat soaring into the dirt. Billy won easily.

"Never mind," Chucky said. "Can I play against you?"

"You're Chucky, right?" Billy asked. "From math class. You sit behind Kendra Collins?"

"Yeah," he nodded. "And you're Billy, the uh- "

"Billy the New Kid, yeah," he said. "Isn't that original."

"And I'm Matt!" a voice called from behind them. The boys turned. "I mean, I used to be the new kid. Last summer, right Chuck? Sucks, right?"

Silence from the peanut gallery. Billy was now on his way to fight the biggie, the tough guy...M. Bison.

"What do you guys want with me?" asked Billy. "The only thing I do is games and hockey. I don't have any money, okay? I don't want to fight you guys or -"

The boys were confused.

"What do you mean you 'don't want to fight?'" Matt said. "Who said that?"

"I've seen you guys following me. Outside my house. In the hallways at school. Now you're here. Just leave me alone, okay?"

Matt looked at Chucky and almost burst out laughing. But he didn't.

"Hold on, Billy. We weren't like, stalking you, or anything," said Chucky.

"We were...are curious. See, two of our closest friends just moved away, and they lived on Tyler Street, too. Now you're living over there - and that can't be a coincidence, right? - and we figured that we're in the same grade, and you haven't made an allegiance to The Sox, and you don't seem to have any horns growing out of your head - as far as I can tell - and you kick ass at Street Fighter."

"We know that you're lonely. That you're the new kid. You don't have any friends. That maybe you'd want some, and that we could be those kids," Matt finished.

Billy looked back at the machine. He had forgotten he had been playing, so his character had lost both rounds. The screen showed a countdown clock alerting him to INSERT QUARTER TO CONTINUE - 10 - 9 - 8 - 7 - 6...

"Wow," Billy said.

5 - 4 - 3 - 2...

"You guys like, rehearsed that or something?"

Chapter Six

Eventually, winter came, and the boys discovered that Billy Shaw was a "hockey kid." They would always stress it that way when they spoke the words, so you could hear the quotations. Matt was an obvious no-go with his bum leg and Chucky never bothered to ask his parents for anything that involved pads - too expensive. For some reason, they had some ingrained ability to know certain things about themselves. It was an unspoken fact that kids are a hell of a lot smarter than most adults give them credit for, and the Gang knew that none of them were living-on-the-streets poor, but they all knew the difference between the West side of Reedy Pond, where you could find used Toyotas and Mercs and pick-ups, and the East side which was most Volvos and Saabs. West side families lived in tract houses built during the Postwar Boom or big, run-down turn-of-the-centuries that adorned large crabgrass yards with the occasional cedar or elm. East side was McMansions. Hell, Joey Lancaster had a paved streethockey rink in his backyard. West side families were mostly blue-collar, voc-and-trade townies. East side was Old Money, or worse, New Money. The Gang lived on the West side, and though Matt's dad worked on State Street for a big financial firm, Matt knew that the fighting he heard most nights when his folks thought he was asleep was about his accident. He didn't have to be told they couldn't afford Christmas presents let alone vacations. They were paying to keep a roof over his head. And he was grateful.

Billy played goalie. Being a big kid already, he was enormous once he strapped on his gear. Chucky and Matt rarely went to his games, though, as the rink was two towns over, and a hockey rink is just so damn cold. But they had a decent snack bar, so when they could catch a ride with Billy's dad, they'd go for the rink pizza alone.

Matt had tagged along to watch a scrimmage against the Saugus team. Billy did really good, only letting one get past. Billy sure was a good goalie. It was early January when they discovered Billy was also good at causing trouble.

———

"Holy shit," Matt said. They had been sitting in the school cafeteria. Chucky, Matt, and Billy. Billy was holding his knapsack in his lap like you would swaddle a baby, or like you wanted to hide its contents from prying eyes.

"Christ, man. Is that shit for real?" echoed Chucky.

Vice Principal Edwards, who pulled lunch duty, had a strict no-cussin' policy. If caught, you were forced to help the lunch ladies clean the grease traps over summer vacation. Fortunately, the cafeteria was noisy this afternoon. It was hamburger day, according to the school lunch menu, but the sad gray pucks on Billy's tray made Matt glad his mom packed bologna.

"Dude, you're staring right at it," Billy said. What *it* was, next to the brown paper wrapped social studies and algebra textbooks, was a pair of professional grade road-ready bright orange spray cans. His dad worked for the Department of Public Works and used the paint to mark where water mains and sewer systems go. "Hocked 'em from my dad over the weekend. Didn't even notice. Also, these." He slowly pulled out a pack of Winstons, just enough so they could see the label. No use showing em off if you were going to get expelled. The contraband was magic to the boys.

"But I don't smoke," Matt said sheepishly. The others looked at him, Billy grimaced.

"Dude," Billy said. And then again, "*Dude.*"

———

As stressed previously, Reedy Pond could be considered a cartographer's nightmare as none of the street's names were apt descriptors. Main Street, a run-down biway with few shops, ran along Canal Street. Reedy Pond had no canal but did have a reservoir on *Forest Drive*. There was Maple Hill, Maple Way, Maple Place, and East Maple. East Maple what? No idea. And all of them were loaded with pine trees. Cedar Street went down near Walnut before creeping up and merging into barren rock-scape known as Walnut Hill. Most of the streets had their loops and turns, forks and one-ways typical of your average post-agricultural New England town. Except for Green Street. Green Street was a perfectly straight line that shot from the North end of town to the South. If you looked at a map of Reedy Pond tipped on its side it would look eerily like the state of Virginia, with Green Street being its southern border, even though it was really the Western border. Just beyond the trees would be a few dozen yards of brush, and beyond that, the railroad. And beyond that...

———

It can be argued that correlation does not equal causation, but on a cold afternoon in 1996, it seemed to double down in spades. The boys were layered in pullovers, thermals, gloves, hand-me-down peacoats; it is cold New England, sun shining bright off the frozen banks, numb cheeks, raw cold. The bridge provides enough shelter from the wind and, as luck would have it, the muck in the fields had frozen solid so the boys have no trouble sliding down the embankment of ice.

Their hideout under the bridge spanned twenty feet on either side from each set of tracks. This was plenty of room for the boys to fool around and gave ample warning if the commuter rail was on its way. They hear the rumble and then the horn of the oncoming train, wait patiently for it to pass before emerging with their wares.

Billy opens his pack of Winstons and hands them out.

"Got a light?" Chucky asks.

"Yeah," Billy says, "I do. Some matches." He feels in his left pocket, and then switches hands. His right hand emerges with a pack of kitchen matches. They light their cigarettes, though it takes Matt three tries - it's too damn windy. Matt, who had never before even thought of smoking a cigarette lest he be smote by the gods (or worse, his mother) shoves the filter onto his chapped lips, causing it to tear a strip of wincing red. And before either Billy or Chucky can light up, he took a haul so deep that he immediately coughed, choking on the blue smoke.

Chucky and Billy erupted in laughter.

"First time?" Billy squeaks, patting his friend on the back.

"Tastes like a dishrag," Matt says through red eyes.

"Winstons taste good like a dishrag should," Billy says, and now they are all laughing. For a second, it looks to Chucky like Matt's going to hurl. But still, he continues to puff until his knuckle is burned at the filter.

When they are finished with their smokes, Billy pulls out the rattle-cans. There is the hollow sound of the shake-shake-shake.

"Who's first?"

There's a silence among them. Matt is bouncing from one foot to the next just trying to keep warm. No one is going for the paint. These were good students, good kids; suddenly it felt like their rebellious streak was inauthentic. And then Chucky grabs the can.

"Fuck," he says.

"What's wrong?" Billy asks.

"No, nothing. I know what I'm gonna do."

BOYS, BROKEN

Confused, Matt and Billy follow Chucky to the underside of the bridge, long coated with years-deep tags from graffiti past, where he shook the can and started spraying, the familiar *SSSS* sound, the scent - overwhelmingly chemical in the winter air - floats not unlike a kite. After a few seconds he steps back and gazes upon his creation.

"The fuck is that?" Matty asks. What he was looking at appeared to be some kind of twisted stick figure and some writing - nothing intelligible.

"It's supposed to be Corey Whitaker. See the sign? It says, 'Village Idiot' on the sign."

The other two inch across the gravel. Billy squints up close. "Meh, I don't see it," Billy says. Matt leans in to get a better view.

"Ditto. But you know what would really get the message across?"

He walks over and grabs the can from Chucky. His sprays are longer, more focused. After nearly a minute, a large patch clearly states in bright orange "FUCK COREY WHITAKER."

―――

Allie was getting impatient. She was in the same chair she had been in for four hours, the last of which had been spent alone since Matt was still with the doctor. She hadn't received an update from Sailor Jerry or Nurse Ratched or anyone and she really wanted to go out for a cigarette but remembered that her good pack was in the freezer at home.

Then she remembered the pack of Winstons she found in the glove box earlier in the day and thought Man, could I use one or two or twelve of those. She finished this thought as Dr. Baxter was returning to the room, *sans* Matt. He entered the room, pivoted and shut the door in one motion.

"Okay, Mrs. Rode," he began, and she stood up.

"Where is he? And for chrissakes call me Allie."

"Okay, Allie. He said that is how he refers to you." Baxter said under his breath. "Listen, Allie -"

"Watch your tone, Doctor. I apologize if I sound curt, but I just want to know what you're doing to help my husband. Where is he? Tell me!"

Baxter paused, reached for a chair and sat. After a long moment, Allie sat back down.

"Mrs. -" he began. "Allie, Matthew is a Section 12. He - "

"Yes, I know. We've been over this before. Why doesn't anyone tell us anything new?"

Again, the doctor paused, as if trying to make his case, but then realized it didn't matter. He had the final say. "He tried to kill himself, and after speaking with him, seeing how he interacted with the staff, we feel he may be a danger to himself, or possibly you or your family."

The lights flickered quickly and for a moment Allie saw an aura. *Fuck*, she thought, *a migraine. On top of this?* She began to rub her temples in a counterclockwise motion. When she looked up at the doctor, fresh tears had formed in the wells of her eyes.

"Please. That's horseshit. Please, when can I see him. When can I take him home?"

The walk home is cold. There isn't much talking, but Billy and Chucky each have another cigarette. The weekend comes, and then school. Billy doesn't come back for three days.

If it wasn't for the essay on *Lord of the Flies* that kept Matt in his room for the better part of the afternoon Monday and Tuesday, he might not have noticed. But Chucky knew something was up the moment he saw Adam Baumer leaving for hockey practice. Adam also lived on Tyler Street but never got along with Chucky - nothing personal, they just ran in different crowds. Billy always got a ride to practice with Adam, so when he saw him solo on Monday a lump grew in his stomach. He asked him if Billy had been to practice.

"No dice," Adam said. "And Coach is pissed, too. Feltzer couldn't stop a puck if he was covered in duct-tape."

Chucky believed this. "Colin Feltzer? Aw, Billy's gonna lose his shit."

While he and Matt were certainly not athletic, they were wunderkinds compared to Colin Feltzer, whose parents made him sign up for anything that would take him, like they were really throwing it out there to see what would stick. Unfortunately for Colin, he took their persistence as his parents legitimizing his talent. And with Billy out, it appeared Feltzer had to fill in. There goes the season.

"Shit," Matt said when Chucky broke the news. They were at Matt's locker, swapping Pre-Algebra for "History of the United States - 1492-1776." Matt closed his locker, twisted the dial, zipped up his bag. "We gotta check on him. I mean, what if it's bad? I swung by his house to drop off his homework yesterday, and you know what?"

Chucky shook his head.

"No answer. I had to leave it in between the screen door."

"All right," Chucky said. "Meet here after class. We'll stop by together."

Matt walked towards history class all the meanwhile praying that his friend was okay. This notion of religion suddenly caused him to remember their test on the Salem Witch Trials, which he of course hadn't studied for. He felt like he was being crushed like Giles Corey. "Aw, shit," he muttered, and entered the class.

―――

When the guys had been having their fun with their orange caveman drawings, what they didn't know was that Lydia Harrington's septic tanked had backed up into her basement. Since it was a busy season for frozen pipes, her septic company, United Septic in Walton Park, had received numerous complaints of similar incidents. The saying "it's a crappy job but someone has to do it" may have come to the mind of Jimmy Proulx, the lone technician for United, who was backed up with calls and told Mrs. Harrington it could take him at least a week to get to her. She was told the same by the two plumbers in town. Desperate, she turned to the Department of Public Works, the only other people she knew in town that may have a solution.

If the boys had been listening while they spray painted "Fuck Corey Whitaker" on the underside of the Tyler Street Bridge, they might have heard a rustling in the thicket behind Lydia Harrington's leach field. They would have seen Vic Shaw, Billy's father, doing overtime for that poor old lady with no one to help her, and what did he see? His son with those kids, that gimp kid and the foul-mouthed ginger, and were they? - oh, yes - they were smoking!

Billy walked through the door and it was a quick backhand across the face - he is shocked, confused. He hadn't had a chance to remove his hat or jacket.

"I saw you!" Vic shouts, then crosses with a right, sending Billy to the ground. "Saw you with those kids!" He kicks his son, now on all fours, directly in the solar plexus. Billy heaves but doesn't throw up. No, that would come later. Right now, it was black and blue and stars. "Spray paint? *My* spray paint? Do you realize I could lose my fucking job over this?" Billy had to get up, get out of this situation, but can't will the strength to stand.

"Errrg," Vic mumble-slurs and shoves Billy into the sink cabinet. If he had been standing, Billy would have gone kidney first into the corner formica, which would have been ugly. But he hadn't, so he fell back on his arm, twisting it crudely behind his back. It made a tearing sound and the pain was bright and immediate, but he couldn't worry about that. Wouldn't. Acting on instinct, Billy opens the sink cabinet and grabs any can or bottle he can lay his hands on and at once, Vic is being peppered with cans of Drano, six-packs of sponges, bottles of dish soap. Besides distracting him, this does nothing but piss Vic off more. He stumbles towards the corner of the kitchen, picks up the microwave and -

BOYS, BROKEN

"-threw it at me," Billy is crying as he finishes the story. They had been sitting in Chucky's basement, where they went after finally going to Billy's after class. Billy broke into his story while they were playing a game of *Risk*. Matt had all of Australia and was in the process of trying for a land-grab of Asia, Chucky's territory. In between his telling, Billy had conquered all of North America. "But he missed. Damn thing was still plugged in, so it just ripped out the faceplate. He was so mad about that."

He sniffed in his tears, laughed a quiet throwaway sound.

"That's how I ran. Had time to run away."

"Lucky for you." Matt says and they stare at him. "I mean, Jesus, Billy I didn't mean it like that."

"It's okay, Matty," he says between sniffles. "I'm so dumb. I'm so fucking dumb." And then the tears start up again.

"No," Chucky say, putting an arm around his shoulder. "Billy, this wasn't your fault. Your dad, I mean, Jesus, man. The guys a maniac. Anyone with a knack for beating up kids, well. There's a special place in hell for them, right? What he did to you? He should be in jail." Billy looked at Chucky in the same way a puppy looks at his owner when he just fed him after two days of forgetting.

"Thanks, man," he said.

"Chucky!"

It was Cat calling from the top of the stairs. For some reason lately, Matt thought, she had spent less and less time with the boys.

"What is it, Brat?" he called back.

"Mom needs to talk to you."

They cross paths on the steps, and Cat sits next to Billy who immediately wipes his eyes and tries to sit up, wincing an ugly face that Matt doesn't particularly care for. If only he could have been there. *But then again*, he thinks, *what good would I have done*?

Cat took the dice and rolled for Chucky. When they played *Risk*, a game with seemingly no end, whenever someone went missing the rest of the players would roll for that person. And they would always play in each other's best interest. "I'm going to build up," she says, adding more armies to Japan.

A few minutes go by and the kids can hear muffled arguing coming from the kitchen. Cat, who had started her journey into adolescence had begun to look more than just pretty, Matt thinks. He then thought of what her hair would feel like through his fingers. When she got older, he knew she would break a lot of guys hearts, and at once felt ashamed for some reason.

"You got Aronson this year, right?"

She grabs a handful of popcorn and cozies up between the boys. "Yeah, but she's calmed down a bunch. I mean, she doesn't seem like the horror story you guys made her out to be." She tossed a few kernels into her mouth, wiped her hand on her dress. "But maybe I have different expectations."

Billy is quiet. He looks like a dog kicked so many times he doesn't even know if he deserves it or not. His crying stopped when Cat came down, but nothing could hide his raw, puffy face and eyes.

The door to the basement opens, and they await the thump-thump-thump of Chucky's footsteps, but they do not come. Instead, they hear someone else.

"Billy?"

It was Mrs. Dawson.

"Billy, could you come up here, please?"

―――

Billy speaks to the police for an hour, is examined quickly. The arguing they heard was between Chucky, who didn't want Billy to get into any more trouble than he already was (and by proxy, Matt and Chucky), and his father, who had no respect for punks who hit kids. Chucky would have found this last statement compelling, since his father was rumored to have beat the piss out of him a few times.

But here he was, calling the cops, a crusader for children. *Guess it doesn't count if it's his own kid*, Chucky thought.

If Vic Shaw had been a townie, the cops may have let it slide, as terrible as that sounds. Detective Kevin Johnson was known to spend most of his nights when not on duty drinking at one of the town's dives after work, and most certainly would have built a rapport with Billy's father. But as Vic Shaw was new to town, and not yet "in the club," spent a single night in lock-up, no bail, and was released just in time to report to work the next morning to get a better handle on Lydia Harrington's pipes.

Later over pork chops with his father, Matt counts himself blessed. *My god*, he thinks. *I've had a rough time every so often, but dad's usually all bark. He's too tired to get physical, Christ. Billy could have been killed. Billy could have died.*

Billy's arm was in a sling for the rest of the hockey season. Worse were his ribs which were cracked due to the cabinet collision. He was taped up, but there was little else that could be done. Every breath was agony.

Chucky and Matt were explaining to his sister about their escapades with the spray paint and how it felt like a good idea, at first. Chucky rolled against Cat (Northern versus Southern Europe), and lost, so now Cat - or really, Billy - had complete control of Europe. This was good news, as it awarded extra armies. They would soon find out that they would need all the extra armies they could get.

"Where is my husband?" Allison Rode is not asking, now. There is nothing polite in her voice. She's been in this cramped ER room for most of the goddamned day and she was sick and tired of the doctor and the nurse and Sailor Jerry. She wanted to go home, *needed* to go home. Some lady in a pantsuit knocked on the door and Baxter let her in. I bet you a million bucks she's a social worker, she thought to no one.

"Hello, Mrs. Rode, I'm Rebecca Stone. I work for the hospital in an outreach, coordinating capacity, and -"

"You're a social worker, right?"

"Well, yes, among other things."

But at this point it doesn't matter. Allie isn't listening to a word she says. She just thinks BINGO and slowly begins to count the cool mil in increments of twenty. She hears, but doesn't listen, as the social worker explains that suicidal tendencies aren't completely unusual, and that her husband did the right thing by checking himself in today, and that, Mrs. Rode, this really is for the best and -

"Please, will someone just call me Allie! Or fucking Allison. Or Al. *Mrs Rode*, god love her, is a wheelchair bound control freak that never gave her only child a set of wings. I am *not* her! Please. Allie."

She hadn't snapped like that in a long time. It felt good to get that off her chest. She didn't like to be mean, but she really knew how to pick her words when she needed to, and right now, with all of this, she needed to.

"Wish I had a cigarette," she finished. "But I know you wouldn't approve."

"Approve, no" said Baxter. "But you'd be surprised how many smokers there are in the hospital. Other stuff, too. Booze, mostly."

He said this as if he were trying to relate. It didn't work.

"Let's get back to the topic at hand," Becky the Social Worker said.

"It can be a stressful environment, is all," said Baxter.

"I bet," Allie Rode said. She didn't like this man, she didn't like this situation at all, but she was trying to see it from the other perspective. Matt had gotten them into a bit of a pickle to be fair, and she really just needed to figure out how to get out of this. Her. Matt. Gabriel. Everyone else could go screw, she thought. Everyone else could -

BOYS, BROKEN

She screamed.

Matt, she could see, was at the end of the hallway on what appeared to be a stretcher or gurney. He was still in his scrubs. Still had on those booties with the textured bottoms. But his *arms*, his arms were tied at his sides. He was being *restrained*.

"Matt!" she called down the hallway, her feet not catching up with her brain as fast as she would have liked, only beginning with a slow one-two-one-two instead of an all-out dash. "Matt, where are they - Where are you taking him?"

Matt didn't like this at all. The straps were chafing against his shoulders and all he really wanted - besides the whole part about not being tied down against his will - was a cigarette from that poor crumpled mess in his jeans which were now in a garbage bag hanging over the stretcher. So close, yet so far.

(Gonna get you New kid – fuckstick – pukeface)

He heard Allison yelling from down the hall.

"Allie," he cried. "They're taking me!" he shouted as two EMTs, one young guy probably just out of college, the other an older, tougher looking mid-forties lady who probably had an inch or two on Matt, began to fold up the stretcher.

"Ready?" lady said to the guy.

"Ah-yuh," he responded. "On two?"

Before he could finish the count, the doors were being closed. Through the window at his feet he saw his wife, Allison, Mother of his Child, Allison, Light in the Storm, Allison. She was just a kid when they met back in college. She stood next to a man pumping fistfuls of quarters into an Addams Family pinball machine, the lights barely blinking, the back display broken so you couldn't feel the rush of the multiball. And he was playing so poorly that Matt thought he could have saved the change for books for his calculus lectures; the guy clearly wasn't an econ major. She was drinking a

Miller High Life and wearing a t-shirt for some band Matt had never heard of called Television. And when he later found out the guy was just a theater partner, and not at all interested in the opposite gender, his gaze relaxed.

When they first made love, he remembered that her dorm was meticulously neat, her jersey sheets warm and as inviting as her naked body. He learned that she was originally from the curiously named Jamaica Plain, a neighborhood of Boston that seemed to be split between the extreme upper-middle class, and a legion of sad poverty-stricken families with hardly a chance of upward mobility. She came from somewhere in between the two and chose the same small liberal arts college that Matt had transferred to for much the same reasons as he did- it was the farthest place from home with in-state tuition.

They were married after graduation and lived childless for years, planning on travelling the world, or at least, paying off their student loans before settling. But as with most things, it seems, life happened, and they welcomed Gabriel into the world. And he was perfect. And they had been so, so good.

And here she was, now, fading from him as the ambulance pulled onto Storrow Drive and Matt began a journey into territory he was absolutely terrified to unearth. Everything he thought he'd ever need or know, or love was now behind him, fading. Going, going, gone.

Part Two:

Windows and Doorways

Chapter Seven

Knott's Haven Institute for Psychiatry was founded in a quiet rural suburb on the outskirts of Boston, Massachusetts in the winter of 1891. Dr. Alexander Fyodor Knott, said to be a genius by some, a fool by others, based his design not on the Kirkbride Plan - focusing on the batwing-like architecture, everything flowing from a central hub - but on a university approach. Knott wanted to distinguish his center from other area asylums of the time, and he wanted to give his clientele, most notably the successful and wealthy types from Cambridge and Wellesley a familiar and comfortable surrounding. With the notion in mind, The Campus, as Knott would always refer to it, was a masterwork in modern medicine. Not only would every building - there were over thirty of varying size - house an on-call physician, psychiatrist, and nurse - each building would specialize and cater to a specific diagnosis as needed. Gone were the days of cramming the lunatics in with the depressives, the motley with the comatose, he would be quoted as saying. This was, to some, a revolutionary way of thinking at the time.

"There will be no padded rooms or straight jackets on my campus," he was known to opine while smoking a stogie with his Board of Directors. "Every patient will be treated as the man he is."

If looked at from above, the outline of Knott's Haven was a snowflake, a series of tunnels connected the buildings underground. This was to provide ease of access to both patients and staff during inclement weather, or as would become routine, emergencies. One such case occurred in the spring of 1913 when a mid-forties male orderly by the name of Winston Thomas Darling threw a twenty-one year old night nurse by the name of Maryanne Parsons off of the steeple of the Big Building, aptly named because not only was it named after noted local philanthropist J. Allen Big, but because it was also tallest building on campus. It was rumored that Darling had begun having an affair with the young co-ed, only to be spurned, which caused the outrage. Though it was also argued that the affair only had one-way consent, that Ms. Parsons was a devout Catholic who wished to be married to Christ if she hadn't chosen finishing school, and in no way wanted to accept the advances of an orderly. She fell twelve stories and landed on the inner row of wrought-iron fence spikes around the campus rose garden. It was late April, the roses just beginning to bud, her blood dripping on the dirt and blossoms. She landed on the metal so hard that her back bent like the number seven. Her funeral was closed-casket. Mr. Darling, the true hero, would rather have faced his maker than a trial. He ended up impaling his own throat on the shards of the same broken window he had thrown Ms. Parsons from. Dr. Knott, it was rumored, was amazed at the amount of self-control it would have taken to kill oneself in such a barbaric manner.

"Imagine the will power," he wrote in his essay titled "The Acute Psychosis of Modern Sexless Males," published in the *New England Journal of Medicine*. "The utter patience and commitment." Of course, not all agreed with Dr. Knott's assessment. One noted psychiatrist from Hopkins would write to his colleagues that, "if ever in need of mental care while you're up Yankee way, 'Do *not* go to Knott.'"

Bet he was a real splash at parties.

The light flickered red-blue-red-blue on Matt's face, young guy standing at his head awaiting the next order from the lady EMT.

"C'mon."

She motioned them forward. Matt noticed the vines of ivy coiling around the wrought iron lamp posts and fences, up the ancient walls. On top of the roof there appeared a bird of some kind. Was it a chicken? A rooster weathervane? He blinked and it was gone. Perhaps it was never there.

"We're moving," young guy says.

And they were.

―――

If asked later, it was Chucky that showed them how to finish it, but it was Cat that really found it. She had been walking home solo, the guys off on an adventure somewhere - probably not the bridge, though. After Billy had been nearly murdered, they didn't venture down there too often. She would have walked with Nicki, but she had recently moved to a duplex across town in the Green Pines neighborhood. Her parents figured they would live on one side and rent out the other half, cover their mortgage and have a little nest egg set aside. Of course, neither of the girls, as smart as they were, understood word one of this. To Cat, it just sucked that her friend moved farther than she was comfortable with traveling by herself.

And she didn't really mind the walk home, really. She didn't always need to tag along with her brother, calling her Brat all the time. She enjoyed having the time to herself. To think. To daydream. She would giggle to herself while she thought of all the hot guys she saw on the covers of her teen magazines (Mark Paul Whatshisname). Fred Savage was her favorite. He was that kid from that show her parents liked. She didn't particularly have any nostalgia for early seventies Americana, but she had thought he looked cute in that cool movie about videogames she had seen with Chucky, *The Wizard*. Deep down inside, though, she thought she liked Fred Savage because he did resemble Matt Rode in a peculiar way that made her feel...

Well, how did it make her feel?

She wasn't entirely sure, exactly.

Since Christmas she began getting these funny feelings, mostly emotional - she would be having a fine conversation with her father or mother about the most mundane topic you could think of and then someone would say something and out of nowhere she would snap or cry or shout and she didn't mean to, but...

But sometimes, she got these other feelings.

Feelings elsewhere.

A few years ago in Ms. Carmody's health class, they did a section on puberty and growing up and becoming a lady and all that jazz, which to Cat was no surprise. Her brother had the class a year before her and she had snuck reading the pamphlets, so she knew what she was getting into, medically speaking, of course. Even though she knew the names written under the diagrams, it was still confusing. Things looked like mushrooms and tadpoles. What they didn't explain, though, was, well...it was so embarrassing, she thought to herself, and if anyone knew she would never be able to live with herself, but sometimes when she was in the shower and had to wash *down there*, it felt so incredibly (goodbadstrangefunexciting) and she was equally ashamed to admit that she would sometimes continue to wash *down there* when she was fairly certain she was clean. Other instances were when she would volunteer to get the laundry out of the dryer a few minutes before the cycle was over, leaning against that warm shaking, or rubbing against the bedpost when she was folding said laundry -

She saw something.

In the woods that stretched up Walnut Hill, behind Anthony Scolaro's house. Tony was a retired shopkeeper who had died two years earlier, his house a vacant lot. The house had been on the market since he's passed, but no one bought it. Chucky's dad always warned them to avoid Tony's little hobby shop off of Endicott Road, that it was either a front for a loan-shark operation or a kiddie-diddler ring, that neither would have surprised him, and to stay the hell out! But it wasn't in Tony's yard that she saw something. What Cat saw was *through* his yard, in the woods up the hill, and she did what anyone of sound age and mind would do in a situation where you're all alone heading into uncharted territory with no one to scream to for help.

Cat Dawson hopped the fence and ventured into the woods.

"How'd everything go with Mr. Flaherty?" Matt asked. Chucky shut his locker door in an almost slam.

"It went." Chucky had been caught cheating off Angela Wood's science quiz on the periodic table and when confronted, instead of owning up to it, he bullshitted saying he was simply "stretching his eyes." Dr. Flaherty, a tough-as-nails Ph.D who spent the majority of his career rolling over the knuckle heads at city college, who took this job teaching middle school science as a means to coast to retirement, who took absolutely zero shit from some kid like Chucky Dawson, called his bluff.

"Okay, Charles," Flaherty had said. "Stay after class and we'll talk."

At the time, Chucky didn't look pleased to hear the news, and he sure as shit didn't look happy now.

"So? How'd it go?"

He looked at Matt. "He made me recite them." He squinted his eyes as if remembering. "Well, try to - the elements. All of them."

"Okay," Matt said, shrugging his shoulders. "That probably wasn't a problem, though, right? I mean, you know some of 'em. You got a great memory. And we haven't learned all of them yet, so there's no fault in -"

"Nah," he said. He shook his head. "I froze." Chucky didn't so much as pick up but *yank* his backpack around his shoulder and began to walk down the hall. Matt, who hadn't followed at first, shouted "Hold up!" and chased after his friend, their four feet reverberating mice squeaks against the empty hallway tiles.

"I fucking froze, Matt. Just like that, guy waiting for me to say something, anything." He clicks the straps of his pack together, thumbs his hands around them. The smell of the school's hallway was dust and paper and the uncomfortable dry-heat of recycled air; Matt always woke up from his naps in the library with a nose as dry as a Triscuit. "He goes 'Say one, Charles.' Kept calling me that.

Charles. I *hate* that," he continued. "'Just one, Charles, and maybe, *just* maybe I won't fail you.'" They were half-way to the exit now, the fluorescent lights reflecting in the hallway tiles became a mirror-image of endless teen dread. "And I still couldn't do it. I stood there staring at him. I swear my glasses fogged up. Forgot how to breathe. Shit, man, I dunno if I can remember how to, right? Says he'll give me an F *this* week, and if I don't study my ass off and pass the quiz *next* week, he'll have to go to Franklin."

"Oh shit," Matt replied.

Principal Franklin was an ex-Marine who served in Vietnam, personally witnessed his platoon mowed down by a bunch of guerilla fighters in the *Battle of Someone Else's Problem* - as he was very fond of relating to the poor student who had the unfortunate task of winding up in his office - and who loved to torture co-workers with his throaty renditions of "Mustang Sally" at the faculty holiday party every December. Like Flaherty, he also ate kids like Chucky for breakfast.

Given this news, being Chucky's best and closest friend, who knew the only way for him to succeed and not be labeled a no-good-loser-punk for the rest of his middle school career padded him on the back and said "I got the cheat codes for Mortal Kombat III. Wanna try 'em out at my place?"

———

Matthew is not alone now. He knows this because there are people mulling about all around - two young medical assistants (probably just out of school), a nurse, and two other patients - but here, sitting in his medical scrubs and booty socks, he's never felt more alone. Everything is juxtaposed wrong. Nothing that should make sense does. The sodium lights are too bright, the room is too cold for summer, and the loud hum from the ventilator is like screaming in a silent film.

They call this part "intake."

To Matt, the sacrament was psychological torture. The irony wasn't lost on him. He had been in and out of one of the three rooms he's allowed in (hallway, kitchen, bathroom) while his paperwork was being processed. The ambulance arrived at quarter-past-five, and now that he is on his feet and has access to a wall clock, sees that it is closer to ten-thirty and thinks "Gee, my life was certainly different last night."

He's already seen the intake coordinators and the nurse, gone over the same history over and over and over again, just as he did with the coordinators and nurses and doctor in the emergency room. Everyone knows the story. He felt like an animation cell, dozens and dozens of the same drawing ad nauseum. This was all before seven thirty. Or yesterday. Or two days from now. Who the fuck could tell how time passed here? Matt looked up at the coordinator with the purple streaks in her hair.

"Excuse me. Miss?" he says. She looked up from what could possibly be a crossword puzzle. "Do you know how long until I meet with the doctor?"

She looks at him with a questioning shrug and then he realizes she has been wearing earbuds this entire time. Probably listening to podcasts or some teen-lit audiobook. He lifts his hands to his ears and makes a pantomime for her to take out her phones. She nods and removes them.

"Sorry, what were you asking?"

He isn't annoyed. Now he's pissed, but he doesn't shout.

"I asked 'do you know how long until I meet with the doctor?' It's been hours, hours since I arrived. I'm tired. Hungry. Confused. Do you have any idea? Any at all?"

"He's probably busy right now, but should be on his way," she shrugged. "After hours, you know?" She put her earbuds back in.

No, Matt thought, *I don't know. What I do know is that I've just about had it with everyone, and I could take that damn iPhone and smash it with my heel faster than you could call for help.*

BOYS, BROKEN

He wanted to shout, to *fume*. He really did. But he also knew that everything was being recorded. Everything he did was being funneled somewhere. He needed to choose his words wisely if he wanted to make any progress.

"I get it," he said, his emotions suddenly carefree. "I understand. Eh, I'm just tired is all." He yawns, resigned. "Been a long day, and I don't want to fall asleep before -"

"HOLD ON," she says loudly, making a "just a sec" gesture with her hand. "MY PAGER IS GOING OFF, SO-" and realized she was overcompensating her speaking volume with the earbud volume, and for the second time in so many minutes, removed them. "Sorry. He's probably on his way. Should be."

Matthew saunters to a chair by a window and peers out across the night sky, looking at a tall building surrounded by a wrought-iron fence. It was too dark to tell, but he thought he had seen a rose garden. "What's that building?" he asks.

She looks out. "Big, she says. "The Big. It holds some faculty offices. Also, where they perform ECT."

"ECT, like shock treatments? That kind of thing?"

"Sorta, she says. "They'll go over everything with you once you're settled." Her pager goes off again. "Excuse me."

She stands and walks over to the reception office, pulls a key fob from her lanyard and *BZZZZ*. She vanishes like a magician's assistant.

Double doors open and another medical assistant, this one with jet-black hair and scrubs, is wheeling over a patient who looks damn close to infinity. They are in mid-conversation coming down the hall, the assistant nearly screaming into the lady's hearing aid, which is dangling from the side of her ear like a bobber on a line.

"You're just going to wait here for a few minutes, Mrs. Jackson!"

"Reno," Mrs. Jackson replies. "Yes, Miss, I'm going to see Frankie and that colored feller with the eye. They're playing the Sands!" The wheelchair is parked next to Matt. His new neighbor, Mrs. Jackson, it appears, who probably sang the old Pall Mall jingle in her sleep - *Over, Under, A-ro-o-ound and Through/Pall Mall, Deli-vers, Flavor to You!-* looks over to him. "Such a pretty young thing she is. But she'll never find a husband working in a laundry, no! Must call my brother Ennis and have him setup one of his sons for a showing. Homely, his boys are, but they are soon to be titans of industry! Make a fortune in plastics!" It takes him a second, but Matt realizes that she's not necessarily bug-shit, but that of course a hospital of this caliber must have some sort of wing for geriatrics, or senility. Dementia.

He sees Purple-Streaks and Jet-Black coming down the hall, but this time they are accompanied by a graying male that Matt can only assume is the on-call physician. *Finally*, he thinks. The doctor and assistants walk straight to the lady.

"Good evening, Mrs. Jackson," the doctor says.

"Young man, is Sammy going on tonight, or is Dean flying solo?"

"You're in the right place, Mrs. Jackson. Everything will be just fine. If you wouldn't mind my...waitresses here. They will bring you to your, er, seat. Just follow me!" And one of the nurses pushes the wheelchair, and as they enter the double doors, and into a wing Matthew prays he will never need to visit, she calls out.

"Lovely, just splendid."

They were in Chucky's basement playing Mortal Kombat III because Matt's Sega Genesis was acting up. They had been playing for hours. Matt really wanted to see how cool Stryker's fatality was. Stryker - supposedly an ex-riot-cop - would strap a load of plastique to his opponent's chest and *Ka-Boom!* Blood, guts, entrails. Of course, neither Matt nor Chucky were wondering how a riot-cop, let alone ex-riot-cop, would have unlimited access to such armaments in a post-apocalyptic hellscape. One of the new stages, a subway platform, had a cool fatality scene where you could uppercut your opponent through the ceiling, and then he would smash through the opposite ceiling directly onto the train tracks where an oncoming train would -

"Guys, guys, guys!" Cat was bounding, leaping, hurtling down the stairs. Her jeans were covered in mud. Her hands looked filthy like she had been wrestling bears. She was shouting with excitement, a barrage of cursing that would make the Holy Mother blush. "Guys! Holy. Shit. Fuck. I mean, guys. You're never gonna believe- damn- I mean-" She took a breath. "Holy shit!"

"Jesus, the hell's the matter with you?" Chucky shouted, barely looking away from the television set. "I spilled my OK Soda."

She took another breath, and now she was jumping up and down, up and down, like a kid about to throw a fit. In a way, maybe she was.

"Guys…"

"Are you okay? What's wrong? What happened?" Matt asked. Unlike her brother, he was genuinely concerned. But looking at her, he could see she wasn't mad. Or upset. She was excited. Almost euphoric?

"Just come with me and you'll see. Please."

"Brat," Chucky moaned. "We've already got plans. See that book?" He pointed to a periodical a bit thicker than a magazine. "That's the Mortal Kombat III Player's Guide. It cost Matt fifteen bucks at Funcoland, and it has every Fatality, Friendship, Babality, and some other stuff. And we're going to sit here and eat Slim Jim's and Combos and drink soda and go through every single one of these cheat codes. And we aren't gonna stop till we're finished."

Cat looked at Matt and shrugged.

―――

It doesn't make sense when they get there. None of it does. They understood, in *theory*, just what they were looking at, but that still didn't explain the how or why. Cat had brought them to Tony Scolaro's derelict house and after looking around the quiet neighborhood to ensure they were not followed, snuck into his backyard. There, she led them over the fence like she had before. Here, the hill turned from grass to roots and trees, becoming much steeper. Rocks and moss protruded down the slopes.

"Hold on, guys. My leg is killing me." Chucky stopped and turned to Matt. Cat continued slowly, then grabbed a young sapling for support. "Sorry," Matt grunted, panting. "This thing. You know the worst part? That it makes me like, only, a quarter Terminator."

"And, like, two-thirds huge dork," Cat giggled. "But in all seriousness, no apologies, Matty. Just trust me. Wait till you see it.

With that she giggled again like the schoolgirl it was sometimes so easy to forget she was. *Man*, Matt thought, *all of this, everything, is fleeting. In the end, none of us are going to make it.* And he was terrified by such adult thoughts.

Chucky looked at his sister and said "Cat, I really hope you know what you're doing."

"Trust me, Chucky. Please."

He seemed a little annoyed by his sister, but, hey, what else were they doing today?

"Yeah. Sure," he agreed. "Matt? Let's go."

They continued up the hill, higher and higher now. Maples and oaks and pines and rocks covered with lichen. And now, a few minutes later they saw *it*, but *it* couldn't possibly be what they were *actually* seeing.

"Is that -" Chucky began but he didn't need to finish. Because of course it wasn't, couldn't possibly be. But it was. What they were looking at, up in the woods, perched high above the town in no place where it could possibly exist, was a bus. Or, what would have been a school bus years ago. It was one of the miniature kinds, the type normally used for small school districts, or for special education classes. It was painted a flat, charcoal gray instead of the yellow and black they were accustomed to. On the side, painted in bright blues and oranges and greens were the words "Peace Mobile." It was confusing. It was a mystery. It was stunning. It was completely -

BOYS, BROKEN

"Bad ass!" Chucky said.

Matt echoed, "Fuck, I can't believe it. Cat, how did you find this place?"

"It was the mirror," Cat said. The boys understood the words she had said but couldn't possibly make any sense out of them.

All Matt could come up with was, "Huh?"

"The driver's side mirror is still attached," she explained. "I was walking up Walnut and thought I saw a, I dunno, a glimmer? Anyway, if it wasn't for the leaves, I would have missed it, for sure. I know it."

The early New England autumn had already begun taking its prey; the crunching beneath their feet was proof enough. Matt looked out and, whoa! He could see the whole neighborhood. Once summer was in full bloom, the canopy would certainly provide nice cover for their - what? They had pretty much stopped going to the bridge ever since Billy's run-in with his dad. And they didn't like the thought of aimlessly bumbling around town while Whitaker and the rest of the Sox teemed. But this place, Matt continued to think, is a bitch to climb up. My leg has been killing me this whole time, and I almost tripped on some of those roots and how do we get down from here? Still, height had its advantages.

"We could build a fort." Chucky answered to a question nobody asked. It was serendipity. "We could build a whole world."

Matt smiled, looked at Cat who had been grinning the whole time.

"Didn't I tell you this was nuts?"

Chapter Eight

Matt is now upstairs, *on unit*, he will learn. He does not know all the lingo, not just yet. But he will. In time he will. It is now very late. He is shown to his room which reminds him of his freshman year at UNH - two beds on either side, hard grey painted brick walls. Except this time around there will be no Deftones posters. He recognizes his roommate as the other patient in the intake that wasn't waiting for a flight to the Biggest Little City. The man, Asian, in his late fifties he imagines, shakes his head and says, "God, I hope you don't snore." Not threatening. Just resigned. Matt was still taken aback and probably looked like a deer caught in headlights. "Please, just don't snore," he continued. "Haven't slept in two weeks."

He turned to face his side of the room and noticed something odd. There were no pillows on his bed. A guy walks past the door just coming from the shower and says, "Towels outside," as if he knew his predicament. Matt didn't get it at first, but leaning out the door, sees the rack of linens, sheets, and towels out in the hall. The men take some, fold a few times and *voila* - makeshift pillows. *Great,* he thinks. He'd spent the last six years sleeping on a memory foam mattress pad from Kohls. This was going to be a wonder for his sciatica. He sighs and sits at the foot of his bed, his patient uniform scratchy on his thighs. It's late. He is tired. After a while, once the tears have dried, he sleeps.

Breakfast was cafeteria style and simply fine. Pale scrambled eggs that weren't too runny, toast, concentrated orange juice in plastic containers that reminded him of middle school. After, there was an announcement on the overhead that the first group of the day would be meeting in fifteen minutes. He didn't know what that meant, but noticed other patients leave the dining hall and make their way elsewhere. He noticed an older man playing what looked like solitaire. He pulled up a chair.

"Mind?" he asked.

"Have a seat. Please."

He reached out his hand to shake. Matt took it, shook, sat. "Name is Zach Conway. See you're still in your formal wear, I take it?"

Matt was confused until Conway tugged on his own tee-shirt, and then he understood. Everyone else he had seen so far this morning had been wearing normal clothes. Matt still wore the rough gray scrubs.

"Guess I didn't get the memo," Matt said.

"And it's too hard to design an outfit when they are strapping you to a gurney."

There was a pause, quiet, but not uncomfortably so. Matt guessed this was a joke. Zach dealt some cards, placed them where they won, and redealt. Matt reached to his back pocket and pulled out his worn copy of *The Alchemist*.

"What is it, the secret of life. Something like 'to fall seven times and get up eight,'" Conway said immediately.

Matt looked at him agaze.

"Used to teach AP English up in Lowell. Funny how many people skip it based on the title, like it's a science book."

Matt nodded. "Whenever I get - lost," Matt begins. He taps the cover. "I dunno. It helps." He tossed the paperback onto the table, slouched back in his chair.

Conway nodded. He was dressed in a maroon polo shirt and light Dockers. No belt, of course. He was slim, and if pressed, Matt would have guessed late fifties. He was balding, but he had his hair fit with a short high-and-tight cut. He wore a neatly trimmed mustache with short graying beard stubble around his cheeks.

"Hey," Conway said. "Don't worry. If you're 'here' -" he points all around him - "then they haven't won. And you haven't given into fear. Not yet, at least." He shuffles the cards, a smooth riffle that sounds fantastic in an otherwise drab hallway.

"What do you want to play?" Matt asks, and Zach smiles.

"What else," he replies. "Crazy eights?"

Throughout the fall The Gang had managed to turn the school bus and its surroundings into a sort of clubhouse that would have rivaled any they could have dreamt up. Billy and Matt had done a lot of the heavy lifting, while Chucky acted as a sort-of site supervisor, showing everyone where everything needed to go. When it would get muggy, as New England Indian summers tended to get, he would begin pushing his tortoise-shell glasses up his nose as they always slid down from the sweat. A Sisyphean task. Cat assisted with the design, mostly, but not in a color scheme way. But rather, she was the one who had the idea to build a second "storey" on the top of the roof out of pieces of picket fence from Scolaro's yard and palettes from the junkyard near the high school. A roof of discarded linoleum sheets was glued on top with a weather-proof epoxy they had located at the hardware store for five dollars.

The walls of the fort were painted dark to blend in with the trees. Cat would even bring yards of jersey fabric to hang in the busted-out windows creating makeshift curtains. Every once-in-a-while they would venture down to the bridge and scour for other refuse and scraps they couldn't find in the junkyard or thrift stores or attics. The bridge had a very odd assortment of belongings, one being a shopping cart someone seemed to have trekked all the way from Kenyon's Grocers on the other side of town. There were hundreds of old bottles from years past that, when redeemed at the recycling center on Ruddles Ave, became their finances. Milk crates. A couple of plastic lawn chairs. These all, minus the bottles, were donated to their cause up the hill. Usually it was Billy and Chucky who would go, mostly since they could hold their own in the event that any trouble happened to come their way, *and* they could run faster then Matt if need be. He took no offense. In fact, Matt actually preferred spending his autumn afternoons at the fort with Cat, if only for a few hours.

By late autumn it was entirely clear they were onto something. The Shire, as Billy dubbed it, had windows that could open and shut (well, half. The others were sealed up by the curtains), and Chucky managed to fix the lever action on the bus door. They had shelter. They could, in theory, survive out here if need be. Granted, they didn't have heat or electricity, but those were utilities they had no need for. They had blankets and sleeping bags and pillows, all extras from their mothers' attics or bought on the cheap at Salvation Army down on Prescott Way.

On weekends, the kids would lie to their folks, Chucky saying he was staying at Billy's, Matt saying he was with Chucky. Billy didn't give a shit if his dad knew where he was. They would climb the hill with backpacks full of Jolt Cola and Doritos and subs from the convenience store and they would live and play and be kids. Safe. Away from the dangers of the older ones. And Cat, who had ascended into the ranks of middle schooler, would join them. Sometimes she would bring Nickie, but most of the time, she liked going solo. No matter who they were with, the town looked spectacular as the sun set from atop the clearing.

"Check these out," Cat told the guys one humid, sweltering Saturday. In her hand was a sheet of stained-glass decals. Nickie helped her put them on the windows facing the sloping hills; when the sun beamed through the prism, colors cascaded throughout the interior of the bus, turning it not into some 2-ton awkward mystery set upon a hill with a jagged downward slope, but into a place of magic. Inside, with the lights and colors and windows and doorways, Cat felt like she was among the rainbowed flowers of Wonderland.

Matt opened his duffel bag, produced a disposable camera and *CLICK*. He then turned to Cat and said, "Smile."

She did, and the picture was taken.

"Doing a project for English class," Matt said. "I have to document my neighborhood, things that I 'rely on.' You'll have to do it next year, probably."

"Will I?" she asked, and for the first time that fall, Matt noticed how gorgeous she would be in a few years, her fire-red hair, her light Irish cheeks.

"Probably," Matt answered. "Transcendentalists. But you're great at that kind of thing."

"Neato," Billy said, clearly not impressed with the decals.

"Hey!" Matt nearly shouted. "She did a great job. Don't be like that." And for the first time ever, he pushed Billy. And it wasn't a love-tap. He nearly knocked him over. Suddenly he felt the room grow small, their eyes staring at him like a thousand pointed daggers. "I'm...Billy, I'm sorry. I didn't mean-"

But Billy was already walking away. Once outside of the bus, he picked up a handful of stones and began throwing them off the cliff.

"Cat, this is so cool," he doubled back. "I mean, it just looks so. Well. It looks...great."

She smiled, and while the boys talked of the Raw/Nitro Monday Night Wars and the American League Post-Season, she squeezed Matt's hand and thought, *I know I'm going to love you forever*. After the darkness came and the talk of who would win in a battle royale - Scott Steiner or Sting - waned, the bus grew silent and they all slept.

The next morning, they walked down the hill, girls first, then boys, about ten minutes apart. They didn't want to make the mistake of inadvertently running into any of their parents this early, asking questions that would undoubtedly end up with one of them forgetting the inner workings of their ruse. And on a Sunday, sheesh. If that happened, say goodbye to hanging out and especially to campouts at the bus.

The boys wiped the sleep from their faces and headed to Sammy's, an old-school style lunch-counter and soda shop. Sammy's was located on the corner of Central Street and Northern Avenue, right smack downtown, and was run by an ex-hippie named Gus. Why a place owned by a guy named Gus was called Sammy's was above their paygrade. What they did know is they served up an excellent mess of breakfasty-goodness (bacon, sausage, potatoes, two over easy eggs, covered in cheese) that came with toast and an OJ for $3.99, which even a kid, let alone five, could afford. They split two orders. They feasted like royalty. Billy must have been in a better mood; he hogged the toast.

At the same time the Gang was busy deciding who got to dip their bread in the last of the yolks, Corey Whitaker, Danny Johnson, and some of the Sox had discovered Billy's carton of Winston's and the cache of spray cans and had turned the underside of the Tyler Street bridge into a marvel of obscenity. PJ Armstrong, a monster of a kid with eyes so cold he frightened Corey Whitaker, drew what could be considered large and inhuman phalli of various origin and stick figures of non-specific genders fornicating. Plenty of curse words. The real fun started, though, when Danny and Corey had shown up, Corey with half a pint of Beefeater he had hocked from his grandfather's liquor cabinet. They passed the bottle around.

"Tastes like flowers," winced Danny.

PJ rolled out his sleeping bag. They had all brought them. Corey had observed over the past several weeks that the kids had stopped coming down here, which he thought was great. *More time for us,* he thought. *More time for me.*

It was just after six-thirty when Seth had arrived, just off of his shift at the Dunks downtown. He was huffing. No one looked pleased.

"Half hour to get here on your bike?" PJ asked. "Are you fucking serious? It's not even a mile!"

"S-s-s sorry," he said, panting.

"Don't bother," Danny piped up. "Late again, you're out. No ifs or ands or buts. Got that?"

"Sure, Danny, sure," Seth had said. Danny didn't look too impressed. Neither did PJ. Danny winked and suddenly Seth was on the ground. He hadn't calculated that Corey was behind him waiting for the signal to take him down, which he obliged. Danny jumped on top of him, his breath reeking of Listerine and berries.

"I said if you're late again, you're just another lame-duck faggot like everyone else, all right you numb fuck?" He slammed his fist into the dirt right by Seth's face, punching a knuckle-shaped hole in the brown dust. Seth looked terrified. Confused. Everyone else was laughing. Everyone but Danny, who stands up after what seems like an eternity, and spits a wad of phlegm at Seth without taking his eyes off him.

Jesus Christ thinks Seth. *I don't know if I can handle this. With friends like these...*

Fifteen minutes later the cat showed up and everything else went to hell.

Lydia Harrington didn't really live alone in that big old house with the big backyard the boys would sneak through, no. Since the spring of 1985 she had shared her home with her one true love, Mr. Brown, a patchwork calico who loved table scraps, especially if they came from Lydia's Famous Roast Chicken, a recipe she perfected over the years by putting pats of thyme and sage compound butter under the bird's skin before leaving it to dry out in the fridge. The skin, which was Mr. Brown's absolute favorite, was not only crispy, but cooked in a succulent mix of juices and fats that made him lick his chops just thinking about it. And he knew - if cats *can* really ever know something - that tonight would be another delicious chicken for two reasons. One, his Person Lady had been wearing one of her funny hats on her head that she only wore on the days she made the chicken. And two, he could just tell in his gut that tonight, he was going to have the best meal he'd ever had, one for the record books, you can quote me on that.

When Lydia had left for church, wearing her big once-a-week hat, she remembered her keys, she remembered her wallet, she remembered to take the trash out. What she didn't remember was to shut the screen door all of the way, and in an old Yankee barn house, old doors are known to swing open and *thatch-thatch-thatch* against the side of the house at night, through the wooing ghost sounds of autumn wind through trees.

On the last day of his life, Mr. Brown awoke to a smell. He noticed, among the house's many scents, that this one was phenomenal, and he couldn't possibly wait for his Person Lady to arrive before seeing what it was. He followed his nose like the old commercial said and ended up at the screen door in the kitchen, facing the backyard. *Okay,* the beast thought. *The smell must be coming from out there,* which was the garage, which was where the trash cans were kept.

He leaned against the door like he would do when his Person Lady came home, but this time, instead of nudging it like he would when he walked between her legs when it was time to feed him or change his water, the door opened. And now he was outside. The possibilities now were endless!

Here he was perched atop aluminum garbage cans full of large bags made of white plastic. He ambled to and fro and CRASH - the can fell over. And the smell! It was a marvel. He pawed and tore at the plastic until liquid and grease seeped through the tattered shreds and began to feed. There was some good (chicken bones with bits of meat attached, cat food cans with leftover chunks), and some things he didn't particularly care for (coffee filters, egg shells). He ate his snack quickly and, sated, he turned back towards the house and meowed to the screen door.

There was no answer.

Maybe she didn't hear me, thought the cat in the way cats do think if they can. He meowed again and again, but still; his Person Lady did not come. He tried to push the door open but being a cat and not having the faculties to understand the mechanics of modern latch systems, was at a loss.

Mr. Brown had been an indoor cat his entire life. He had only managed a few handfuls of the outside and those glorious scents when his Person Lady opened the door for the few seconds it took to enter and exit the house. Now, his Person Lady gone for all he knew, he was on his own. And now he could experience the field behind the house, the field with all its marvelous aromas and sounds. Not a bad deal.

Mr. Brown darted into the meadow and - what was that? He heard a *thump-thump-thump* and pounced through the brush to discover a nice sized jackrabbit. For Mr. Brown, the chase was on.

The rabbit was scared for its life and did the only thing it could do when confronted with the daily monsters seeking to prey on him. He ran the fuck away. *Lefts, rights, ups, downs, overs, unders, around the bends, down down down the steep slopes and gravel and metal and four tall human-boys and dirt and up up up and the Hole find the Hole and Safe Safe Safe.*

Mr. Brown couldn't make it up the hill. That rabbit was really fast and the fact he had been living off table scraps for the past ten years had really put the kibosh on his track record. The chase was over, and he had lost, but - what was this? He turned towards other noises - mumbling, Person sounds - and saw four Person Boys!

BOYS, BROKEN

"Holy shit!" PJ had said when it was first unsheathed. "Looks like something Rambo would have." The survival knife had a razor-sharp blade and serrated back so you could perform various tasks needed to survive in the elements - hence the name. The bottom of the handle unscrewed and became a compass; the inner sleeve of the handle was hollow to store a folded map, or a flint and steel to start a fire. Ken Armstrong, a former US Army Ranger and PJ's uncle, bestowed the tool to his nephew just two months prior for the boy's fourteenth birthday.

"Careful with it," he said. "This is a damn serious knife. You need to make sure you are responsible with it at all times. And I don't want to hear from my sister that her son got suspended for doing something stupid like carving his name in a cafeteria table or some dumb-nut shit."

"Of course."

"And don't go messing around with it. This is a tool. I've had it since Georgetown and believe me. Those were some of the toughest sixty-one days of my life. But I got through it. And maybe someday you will, too."

He hugged his nephew, not knowing that PJ had already begun shooting BBs at neighborhood pets from his wrist-rocket slingshot, a feat that no-doubt would disqualify him from ever passing the exam at the MEPS in Southie. And if Charlie Strong, his Boy Scout troop leader, knew what he was about to do, PJ would certainly lose his whittling chip.

And now, here he is, standing over Mr. Brown, and the cat has no idea, none whatsoever. If he did, he would have run back into that field, back to the garage, back to the good smells and warmth of his Person Lady.

But Mr. Brown didn't know. He was just a fucking cat.

"Here kitty, kitty," PJ said. He points to Seth. "Hey, new boy! You got dibs."

Mr. Brown gave his final meow and nestled up to the boy's legs. They all take turns, but it is PJ who brought the knife.

Matt and Cat split from the rest of the group as they left the diner. Billy, Nickie, and Chucky were going to see if there was anything else they could scrounge for at the junkyard, and if not, just bum around in the warm September breeze. Maybe they could head down to the lake, take a quick dip from the shore behind the cemetery. It was starting to look like one of those perfect Massachusetts days where you could almost taste the apple pies baking in the neighboring houses. It didn't feel like a Sunday, with the dread of homework and Monday's new assignments. It felt, well, *right*.

They walked for a while, Cat's feet tripping into an awkward cadence attempting to match Matt's rhythm, causing them to slow to a snail's pace. They didn't notice because no one ever does. It's just one of those events that happen when you are in the first thralls of - what, infatuation? A crush? Matt didn't know, but he liked the walk and he enjoyed the company.

Birds chirped.

"Thank you," Cat said, her words breaking the silence. "About the glass."

"The stained-glass?" he answered.

Matt blushed, though Cat didn't see. She was looking at her feet, kicking pebbles, which was fine by him.

"Don't mention it," he said. "You did a great job. And the guys, well." He trailed off, not knowing how to put it in words. He had always been a quiet kid, not shy. But reserved. He didn't say much, and felt like most times, his friends knew what he meant in the few sentences he chose to speak.

"They don't get that it's not always easy," he said. "Being a part of the group."

BOYS, BROKEN

"What do you mean?" she asked him. He stopped and turned to her.

"Like, with my leg, right? It sucks going up that hill. It really does. Man, I can barely walk now without limping. But I do it cause I like being with you guys. With you," he managed. "But I guess I'm not supposed to admit that it's hard sometimes, right? I gotta be cool, I guess. And it isn't easy. And I know it's probably the same for you."

"How so?" she said, her lips curling into a smile. "Tell me."

"Well," he smiled back. "You're like, wicked good at designing stuff, like the windows. But it's not all pretty colors and fabrics for you. I mean, I know that there's something else there. Something else to it. It's like, the other guys, they are strictly thinking 'How will this work,' like in a function kind of way." He paused. "But you see things differently. You know there's more to it. I dunno, maybe I'm not making any sense. I'm just glad that you are part of the group."

If there ever was a time she would have wanted her first kiss, it would have been right there.

They continued walking in silence. The leaves on the trees were bright orange, the kind tourists from all over would travel to every year, which he never understood. *Why do we all go to Boston just to watch the leaves fall down?* he thought.

When they arrived at Tyler Street, Matt stopped suddenly.

"Hold on," he said to Cat. She came to a halt beside him. The bridge was in front of them, they could see it down the road. Everything was still in the quiet Sunday morning. But the bushes beside it - was there something else? He squinted, and then -

"Into the bushes," he barked at her. "Now!"

At this, Cat didn't understand what her friend had ordered, but confused, she ducked into the thicket. Matt disappeared and after reorienting, she couldn't tell if he were a few feet, or a few hundred feet away. But it was quiet among the reeds and shrubs. "What are we," she began.

"*Shhh!*" she heard what could only be a ghost, the noise echoing around her. That's when she saw it.

The chain-link fence on their side of the bridge, the barrier made to keep the damn kids off the damn thing, as her father would have said, appeared as if it were bouncing. And with each tiny bounce, each small recoil, she heard a high-pitched squeak that sounding like a witch's cackle.

Creak. Creak. Creak.

Then she saw a hand. Then another. Someone was scaling up from underneath the bridge. She could hear mumbling and then she saw him, the one of the boys she had feared. Danny Johnson. He was coming out of the ditch, only he wasn't alone. Behind him was Corey, and he was followed by a tall brunette she didn't recognize, and finally by PJ Armstrong, a massive refrigerator of a kid. Armstrong was carrying what looked like to be an olive-green Army issue duffle bag - the bottom appeared soggy, as if it had been sitting in a puddle, but there had been no rain as far as she remembered. They were all laughing and joshing as they pulled each other out of the ditch and started to walk past her. This made Cat nervous, and when she got nervous, she had to pee. Always. This reflex made her shake and try as she might, her shaking caused her to roll her weight onto her left foot, killing some freshly dead leaves in the process, making a beautifully terrible *CRUNCH*.

Danny stopped dead in his tracks.

"What was that?" asked Danny. He threw up one hand in a "halt" sign.

"I heard something, too."

"Seriously?" Corey said. "Probably a squirrel or raccoon or something."

"Nah, man. I *heard* something." Danny stood among the boys and shouted into the trees. "WHO'S OUT THERE?" His words echoed softly, but that was all the noise there was. He looked around, turned in a three-sixty, slowly taking in his surroundings. The other boys looked at each other not knowing where this was going. "I said who THE FUCK is out there?"

There was nothing but the sounds of the woods. Her bladder felt swollen, like a balloon set to burst, but she wasn't going to squeak. She couldn't. She wasn't sure if things would get violent, but they were in too much danger, outnumbered as they were.

"I don't think anyone's there," said the kid Cat didn't recognize.

"And I don't think I gave you permission to speak, numbnuts," Danny replied. "Ya know, Seth, for someone who wants to be part of the group, you really don't seem too interested in knowing your goddamn place."

Seth, she thought. That's his name. Probably Chucky's grade. From her vantage point, Cat could see the boys through the leaves, but not much else.

"Sorry, Danny, I just-"

Then Corey turned, facing her east and pointing. "You gotta be shitting me! Look! It's the gimp!" Corey began laughing.

Oh no, thought Cat. They hadn't even noticed her, but were able to pick out Matt? But how?

The boys were chuckling and whooping to each other like they just won the fucking Mass Millions.

"I Seeee Yoooou," Danny sang. "You got nowhere to run to, Ass Hat. Now why don't you come out here before we come in and drag you out?" He chuckled. "Save me the trouble."

And then she saw Matt as he came into view, slowly at first.

Matt had appeared into her frame through the leaves by entering stage left, not kicking or screaming, but of his own volition. He was immediately met by the wall of boys, not circling, no. They didn't need to sneak around. They knew damn well he was trapped, and so did Matt.

No, no, no! she thought. *What is he doing?*

"You alone?" Corey asked, but Matt didn't say or make a sound. Before he knew it, he was on the ground, his arm locked behind his back. "Let me repeat myself, fuckbitch." Even as surprised as he was with the quick attack, Matt was always surprised at the vocabulary of middle-school kids. The boys were hollering with laughter now. "Are any of your retard friends here with you, or did you make your way out here by yourself?"

He bent Matt's arm higher. He winced but didn't cry out.

"Are you retarded?" Danny screamed at Matt. "We saw what you guys wrote down at the bridge. He's gonna break your arm, Rode." Danny then coughed up a big one and hocked it onto Matt's head.

Cat thinks *Just say you aren't alone. Tell them I'm here. Tell them we were just on our way. We're leaving. They'll let you go. They're really nice guys deep down and they'll let us go, right? WHY DON'T YOU SAY SOMETHING -?*

The snap of the arm sounds like one of the dry twigs next to Cat's feet.

At first there was silence. All of the boys. Cat. Danny. Then the screaming began, first with Matt, and then the cacophony of panic amongst friends, Danny yelling at Corey, who was screaming back, an echo of white accomplishing nothing that was loud enough to break bones. It was during the confusion that Cat ran to her friend's side, which was also when the rioting stopped.

Danny looked at the girl with eyes that seemed inhuman; they had a *witness*.

"*RUN!*" Matt screamed.

And that's exactly what she did.

Chapter Nine

He is sitting with Conway after his first group meeting of the day. Something called Daily Planning. Everyone in the group went around and stated their current mood, a goal they had for the day ("to feel less anxious," or "to finally get some sleep"), and something they wanted to let go of, metaphorically speaking. To Matt, it seemed like everyone here was an old pro, though he knew that by definition, the short-term unit only catered to patients being admitted for a few weeks at a time, so really, he wasn't too far off from anyone else in here.

When it came to be Matt's turn, he introduced himself and said, "My name is Matt. Today I feel...I dunno." He held out his hands in a shrugging-to-the-world motion. "I guess I'm still processing all of this. Like, it feels like the rug has been pulled from under my feet and I'm still tumbling in the air." He stopped and looked at the inquisitive faces in the room. Some looked kind, others apathetic. "I've never done anything like this, so I'm still pretty confused with how this whole thing works. Sorry."

Afterwards, he is sitting with Conway when a sharp-dressed man in Dockers and an expensive looking cornflower-blue button down appears. He is holding a tablet computer in one hand, and a massive case file under the other arm.

"Mr. Rode, I'm Dr. Barry Young, your case worker. Would you please come with me?"

Matt looks at Conway with a "You Mind?" and Conway brushes him off.

"See you when you get back. And I'll play in your best interest," he says.

Yeah, Matt thinks. Just like when we were young.

They aren't alone. Across the room from Matt and Dr. Young sits an Asian man in thick framed glasses, pale yellow shirt. He doesn't stand or shake hands or greet him. On his shirt pocket is an ID badge with his photo and Dr. Tso printed. He is holding a clipboard while Dr. Young listens while Matt pours out his history, again, going into all the details about the car accident, the death of his father, Allison and Gabriel, and work work work. He goes into the ups and downs of his marriage, the cheating that happened on both sides, the fact that neither of them wanted to get married, didn't believe in the concept, but did anyway. He went on and on about how much he loved his son and his family though he never wanted to be a father, and that dammit it was just so hard sometimes. That he went to school to be a teacher, did his dissertation on Chaucer and when the bottom fell out of the market and no universities were hiring because the tenured not dare retire. For two hours it all came out, until there was nothing left.

The door to the suite opened and out walked Matt, Young, and Tso. Matt immediately sat back down with Conway. Just looking at Matt's puffy red eyes, his tired face, gave him all he needed to know. Guy had shit for a poker face.

They sat in silence for a long time.

"He's prescribing me pills. Antidepressants. Some large enough dose so they can measure any side effects."

"That's not abnormal," Conway said.

BOYS, BROKEN

"Can't remember the last time I took anything more than a few painkillers without really needing them. Wisdom teeth, maybe, or the few percs I used to sell in college. But that was like, a dozen years ago. I've never been good on pills."

"Well think of the bright side. If you were on your own, outpatient basis, and they needed to change your meds, you think it would happen in a few hours? Weeks is more like it. Sometimes I think that we're, and forgive me for being blunt, but kind of lucky, in a way. To be in here instead of on our own, right?"

Matt took a long sip from his cold coffee. It tasted like an ashtray, which went a long way coming from a smoker of twenty-odd years. "Breakfast wasn't awful, right?"

"Coffee's shit," Conway relayed, which brought a smile to both of their faces. "Trust me kid, I've been drinking that shit for a long time and it does not grow on you."

"Damn," Matt says. "Today is what, Friday? My wife takes our son to story time at the library and on the way stops to get her cold brew at this great cafe - "

He stops.

Holy shit, he thinks. Allison. After intake, once I came up here, I just went to sleep. Now it's 11:30 and I still haven't -

---

"Thank you for calling Knott's Haven. If you know your party's four-digit extension, please enter it now, followed by the pound sign."

Allie hit zero. She wasn't given the prompt, but she knew that whenever she called corporate and needed to talk to somebody Right-The-Fuck-Now, you just mash your zeroes until someone picks up. It rang exactly twice.

A nasally-sounding voice answered. "Thank you for calling Knott's Haven. This is the operator. How may I direct your call?"

She told the receptionist everything. About her husband being wheeled away, the EMTs, not saying where they were taking him since he hadn't been screened for potential triggers, how she had called the *two* other National Leading Mental Health facilities in the city and the *four* not-top-ranked mental health facilities in the city with no luck before switching to the suburbs.

The receptionist, Martha, had been very patient. But she also stated that due to Federal and State regulations, HIPAA laws, etc, that she could not legally divulge the whereabouts of any patient, could not confirm nor deny the existence of a Matthew Rode as patient or not.

"I know," Allie began, "but I'm, frankly, I'm gonna fucking lose it. I'm sorry. For swearing." She began to sob into the phone. "I'm just so lost and scared and I need to find my-"

Her phone starts vibrating against her face and thinks, "Well, I guess a stroke at thirty-five isn't exactly unheard of" before realizing it was her call waiting. The number, it showed, was the same number she had just dialed.

———

"No!" Matt screamed. He saw Cat run off, Danny and Corey taking chase. He rolled onto his side, which was agony to his dead arm, now resting on his hip. He felt glass in his veins, couldn't remember a pain this bad in a long time.

The lively young saplings and branches worked to Cat's advantage, their elasticity creating a diversion. Her petite size also aided in her escape; she could crawl through the brambles the bigger guys had to avoid, under fallen logs, around tight corners. She managed to get further, not looking back, no, not once looking back, all the while hearing their chants and guttural taunting. She made it to the embankment and froze.

Her feet were at the edge of the run-off, her hands holding onto the roots of a small sapling poking out of the clay. She sat and scooted off the wall doing her best to dig in her heels into the side of the mud. She slowed, stopped, and managed to spin herself in a one-eighty, her hands still grasping the roots of the tree, an anchor that kept her suspended about fifteen feet above the train tracks. She looked as if she were giving the wall of earth a friendly hug. She could hear the boys from above her shouting.

"This way. C'mon!"

PJ and the brunette boy had been left to watch over Matt, but the way the kid looked, all beaten and twisted, they didn't think the gimp would give them any more trouble. The brunette stood, took out a bowie knife, and started to shave bark from a stick. PJ squatted over his duffle bag, opened it, and took out something Matt would have recognized by if blindfolded. The rattle-rattle of a spray can.

"I think I heard her go this way," PJ said. The brunette didn't take his eyes off of his whitling.

"Go ahead, man." And then he added - in a tone that would haunt Matt decades later - "Have fun."

The Sox were smart. They had all made it through the thicket, just at different points. PJ was the closest to Cat, who was about fifty yards from the bridge. *Oh no,* she thought. *My hands*! She began to feel the roots losing their hold in the earth. Just then, her left foot slipped in the clay. She couldn't help it out of the sheer fright of the situation, but she squeaked a yelp of surprise, her hands now the only thing keeping her dangling body attached to the wall.

A head popped over the lip of the cliff.

"I found her! Hey, guys!" It was PJ. "Bitch is over here! Hey, guys!"

And as she heard his voice yelping to his friends in ecstacy that she was discovered, as her mind went to a dark, trembling place and the rest of her bladder finally gave way, when she was completely and utterly terrified of what could possibly be next, that was when the roots gave way and Cat began to slide, kicking her feet like she was walking up a down escalator. Her knee banged against a rock jutting out of the ground and then she was tumbling, rolling, somersaulting down the incline. She landed in an ugly way, sprawled out on her chest with an *Oof!*

She moaned. Her mouth was full of gravel. She spat rocks and blood. The wind had been pushed out of her lungs like deflating balloons. Her vision was blurry and when it refocused, she saw PJ, Danny, Corey. In the distance she could hear screaming, but at this point it could have been a freight train or a robot. She wasn't good with voices.

———

She couldn't see everything. She couldn't remember it all. Images appear like Polaroid photographs - three teens looming over her, her shirt being ripped, falling maple leaves, a wet sensation on her chest, a whippoorwill flying to its nest. She hears laughing and she cries. She hears the chirping birds and she cries. She hears the train whistle and she cries. She closes her eyes and for the first time in her twelve years she prays that they leave her alone, prays to whoever is listening that they don't do *that,* that they leave her alone so she can rest. She opens her eyes and sees that they are gone. It is full dusk.

———

His arm wasn't broken. Danny had underestimated the amount of leverage required. What he did do, though, was dislocate Matt's shoulder for the second time in his life. The pain was a grinding concrete mass of sparkle and shock.

The brunette that Cat didn't recognize was Seth Michaels. He was a pretty good kid. He played centerfield for the Sox and was in the same grade as Matt. And until this day there was never any bad blood between them. They even shared a lab bench in chemistry. Matt had no idea why Seth would be trawling around with these guys who did absolutely nothing but wreak havoc. He also noticed that Seth, believing that Matt was out of commission - which in some ways he was - was biding his time waiting for Johnson or Corey to bark some orders. The sounds of their chase through the woods began to fade.

"You guys okay out there?" he shouted into the expanse of oak and maple. "Let me know if you need any help, guys." He paused, and then, "I'm really good at climbing trees! So, look up! Guys!"

Matty coughed on the ground, could almost taste the moss on the stones. The noise got Seth's attention and when he turned to him, said "Not smart, Matt. Thought you'd have more sense and black-out."

Matt started to roll over, maple leaves stuck to the back of his Wrangler jeans. He attempted to sit up, but by doing this immediately recognized a dilemma. He would need to put his weight on his good arm - which now dislocated became his bad arm. As if reading his thoughts, Seth put down the stick he had shorn, walked over to Matt and simply tripped his arm out from underneath, causing Matt to fall back onto a healthy sized piece of granite.

"Ah!" Matt groaned, and then "why. Why did you do -"

"You guys aren't gonna win this. They found your spray paint. They know it was you guys." He reached into his pocket, pulled out a stick of Juicy Fruit like a gangster would roll a Lucky. "Danny's really pissed, and Corey's pissed. And I just figure I'd rather be on their side, cause I sure as shit wouldn't want to be in your shoes."

He bent down next to Matt as if to tie his shoes and then punched him directly in the hamstring, instant spasm. Matt winced again.

"Okay, okay. How's about this? I help you up, and we'll just fight fair. You and me, okay?" He pulled Matt up by his collar before letting go, his back thud against the rocks, tears began to stream down his dirty cheeks.

"Whoops! Looked like I slipped!" chuckled Seth.

It was the sound of the laughter that finally did it. Matt somehow ignored all of the pain he was feeling, and funneled his energy into sheer rage and violence, and in a flash, shoved both of his size ten sneakers into Seth's torso, causing him to stumble back and sit down hard. Not enough to do any damage, but he took Seth by surprise, and it bought him the time to take all the adrenaline he could muster and force himself to his feet. Seth, who was still in utter shock of what had occurred, scrambled.

"You fucking cheat!" he shouted, running at Matt who, like he was Shawn Michaels on Monday Night Raw, side steps him beautifully, tripping Seth who goes flying into the dirt. "Fair," he mumbles.

Matt is now standing above Seth.

"Fair? You call three guys chasing a girl into the woods fair?"

Somewhere in the distance he heard the echoed call of *"Guys! I found her. Bitch is over here!"*

Matthew Rode looks at Seth Michaels directly in the eye. He raises his foot and sends it kicking Seth across the face. Blood spouts from a nose so broken it would leave a bump on the boy's bridge the rest of his life. Seth wails.

"What, was this your initiation into their gang, Seth?" Matt shouts. "You fucking dick."

Matt climbs on top and punch-punch-punches with his only good hand. They weren't strong jabs, but they connected. Knowing that Cat was off somewhere in danger, knowing he had to end this quick, he did the only thing he could think of. He stared at Seth with an anger he had never felt in his entire life.

"You did this to yourself."

He leapt in the air and came down square on Seth's right kneecap, the audible *POP* sounding like a cap-gun. The birds in the trees took off in flight as if they knew of an oncoming storm.

It was the train's horn that woke her. She wasn't alone. It was later, she could feel that instinctively, but if asked, she would be hard pressed to say how long she had been out. Her body ached. Her skin felt taut and cold and then it hit her that her shirt was missing, her stripped chest exposed to the woods. Well, not entirely *missing*; it had been draped on her chest and fell when she awoke and stirred, so it now resided in her lap. It appeared she was only in white cotton underpants and immediately felt ashamed. But something else. There was something on her. Something sticky.

"They're gone."

It was Matt and he looked like the aftermath of one of those Mortal Kombat games they were always playing. He was knelt down a few feet beside her drawing in the dirt with a bark-shaved stick. "It's spray paint. On your chest. And back."

"How-" she began, but that was all. She tried to sit up and fell back down. The rush of blood caused her to get violently dizzy. "I think I might puke."

"Go ahead," he said, but she didn't. Matt noticed the way the last rays of sun came through on the muss of red hair still covered in pine needles and thought God makes the strangest kinds of beauty.

"I thought they broke your arm," she says after a while. "I swore I heard a -"

"Snap?" he finished.

"It sounded awful."

"Think it's just dislocated again. Probably see a doctor." And then like that, he fell over. Not hard, as he was already sitting on the ground, but tilted on his side.

He is cold when he comes to. He notices he isn't wearing his flannel anymore, just a white undershirt which, in the early evening of autumn, makes his body shake. Looking over, he spies the thief. Cat is wearing the double-thick L.L. Bean, and that's fine by him. Her shirt was ruined. Her body -

He forces himself to his feet, his shoulder a swollen wreck. If they had a mirror, they would notice that they both looked like the butt of the joke in the "You Should See The Other Guy" routine. Matt decided there was no way he could hide it this time. This wasn't some boys will be boys' shit. Many bodies left today broken.

"I need to get to a doctor."

"But what about your mother?" Cat asks. "Your folks will freak if they knew you were fighting again. Hell, how am I going to explain this to Chucky? To my folks? I don't even know what happened, but I'm colored in Day-glo."

"We weren't fighting," Matt says. "We weren't. We weren't attacked, we weren't in a fight. Nothing like that happened. That's why."

Cat looked at him and decided to grow confused.

"Look," he continued. "I'll say that we were walking around, you and I were just aimlessly enjoying the day and stumbled on the bridge, and that 'yes, we know we're not supposed to play down there,' and I'll say you spotted some rabbits and were chasing after them because they were so goddamn cute, and you misjudged their speed and you tripped and went over the hill. I tried to pull you up, and further misjudging my strength, popped my arm out causing us both to fall. Got the whole story down. Just trying to decide if 'rabbits' sounds better than 'bunnies.' What do you think?"

"That's the stupidest thing I've ever heard. No one will believe it." They walked towards the tracks and started making their way back towards town. "And what about Corey and Johnson? Do you think they'll remember seeing any bunnies? What if they've already gone to their folks?"

"They aren't talking to anyone," Matt says with a shocking amount of balls. "Danny and PJ beat the shit out of me. But what are they gonna say if we went straight to the cops right now, you, covered in spray paint? Maybe molested. What are they going to say? What, that 'we were acting in self-defense from a twelve-year-old girl?' And look over there."

He pointed and her eyes followed, slowly unveiling a nightmare - it was some sort of unidentifiable animal carcass that seemed to have been skinned, lying in the dust and gravel, surrounded by fresh sneaker prints.

He continued. "I don't even think Detective Johnson would know what to make of it. His kid. Fucking sociopath."

So, no cops for either side, it appeared. She looked uncomfortable and grew silent, thinking of the way they looked when she had finally come to after the fall, how they were leaning over her like vultures, whispering things that she couldn't - or mustn't - understand. A dark place inside of her knew exactly what their plans had been, and she was glad when they vanished. She wanted to get out of her head, go home, see Chucky, take a bath. But for the time being, she would go home with Matt.

"You certainly have your story straight, it seems," she peeped. Matt looked at her, then tossed his stick into the woods.

"I've had three hours to come up with it. It's almost dinnertime."

They continued to walk on the tracks, keeping their heads down, listening for train signals, their eyes open, constantly on the lookout for monsters.

Chapter Ten

The buzz of the locked door makes her jump, but as she enters the unit she is immediately taken aback, and she realizes why Matt had told her to bring clothes. *This place is a dorm*, she thinks. All of the patients and staff are sitting around - reading books, coloring, watching TV. There's a mid-twenties guy in the corner playing a hauntingly gorgeous melody in E flat Major on a piano. Everyone is in casual clothes. Jeans, tees, sweats, pajamas. The staff are easily identified by their name badges.

She goes to the reception desk but there's no need. Allie has never had to visit anyone in any type of lock-up situation before, so she is unaware that the patient is informed of the visitor before they are even buzzed into the unit. This leads to fewer altercations, no big scenes of an unwanted family member/friend/co-worker arriving unannounced. Matt is sitting in a rocking chair waiting for her. He stands and she runs to him, embracing for a hug, but he stops her.

"Not allowed," he whispers. "Not in a bad way, but I'll get to that later. Everyone's nice so far. Less *Cuckoo's Nest*, more Sophomore year at State."

"I brought some clothes," she says, holding out a tote. "Even got the fancy socks cause they were on sale. And your razor." But Matt brushes that aside.

"I think I'm gonna let it grow." He then went on to explain about the Sharps Room, a closet that kept all of the razors and contraband, and that if he wanted to shave, he would need to be supervised, and it would become this whole thing. "Beards are in now, right?"

She smiled, if a little uneasy. He continued.

"Just think. It'll almost be sweater weather, and I'll have a jump-start on all the pumpkin-spice hipsters at Starbucks, and who knows, I had breakfast *and* lunch today so if we hit the trifecta with dinner that will be the first time in eight years I can remember eating meals, and breakfast was okay this morning, but if that's the coffee than the filter needs to be soaked because-"

"Honey," she said, touching his shaking arm. "What's going on. Are you okay? Nurse?" She looked around. "Matt, I've never seen you like this."

A young nurse approached.

"He's getting used to his meds. That's all. The doctor gave him a high dose, which is pretty standard. His body is simply reacting to new chemicals in his system. I'm Betty. You are?"

"His wife. I'm his wife, Allison. Allie."

"Okay. That's good. And Matthew, how are you doing?"

"I'm fine," he says, coffee popping over the rim of his styrofoam cup dribbling brown spatters onto the tile. "Just a little jittery."

"Matt," Allie says. "This is not jittery. You are going a mile a minute, and your hands-"

She pointed.

"What?"

"They are visibly shaking like you've been in a meat-locker all night!" she insisted. "Why is that happening? Why is this happening, Betty?"

"Mrs. Rode," she began.

"Please just call me Allie," though she knew she wouldn't. No one ever listened. But she didn't blame Betty. God knows how hard it must be to keep track of all these patients, let alone their families.

"Okay, Allie. Like I said. Sometimes a diagnosis can be vague. Your husband came in with catastrophic depression and suicidal ideations. After discussing with his team, the doctor started him on high doses of antidepressants. The jitters that he is experiencing could be a simple side-effect of his body metabolizing something new."

"Or?"

"Or it could be the coffee," Matt says, and tee-hees a little too loud for the situation.

"But seriously," Betty continues, "We'll need to give it a couple of days. Dr. Tso knows what he's doing. He'll have a better idea by Monday or Tuesday."

"Monday?" Matt shouts suddenly. "I thought - I mean, Tuesday? The forms I signed said forty-eight hours. Today is Friday, right?"

"Forty-eight to seventy-two," Betty says. "And those are *business days,* Mr. Rode. Like I was telling Allie. You need to look at this like a good thing that you are doing. Right, Mrs. Rode?"

She looks at her husband and then to the nurse, but doesn't say anything because as of that moment, she doesn't truly know.

After Allie left, his bag was searched for contraband, Matt was finally bestowed what seemed a bounty - a new pair of Levi's 501s, two black V-neck tee-shirts, two grey crew-neck tees, one pair athletic shorts, one pair pajama pants, one loaf of Pepperidge Farm white bread, one package each of deli bologna and American cheese, underwear, socks, sneakers, and - if he was ever in the mood for some light reading - a copy of Michael Patrick MacDonald's *All Souls*.

He showered and dressed in his new costume and Wow! How refreshing it felt to be in one's own skin. His mood had improved. He was going to find Conway. See if he could finally block his rook's attack.

BOYS, BROKEN

Marcia Rode looks at her son, waits for him to finish his retelling of the day's events, slowly sipping her Johnnie and Ginger (she had been sober for some time, but now that she couldn't drive, well) and quietly sets her glass on the table, and as he gets to the part about the bunnies, slaps him stark across the face. Since she was below him coming at an upward angle, her nails awkwardly scratch across his cheek leaving weeping red slits like a rake across clay. Matt gasped in pain and confusion.

How did the story not work, he thinks. *We practiced it a dozen times.* Cat had even tried to help him make a sling with some duct tape and a curtain from the fort.

"Just shut up, Matt, will ya," she says, the booze bringing out her slight accent. "Can't bullshit a bullshitter."

"But mom," he says, and she pushes him back. Her wheelchair isn't locked, so she moves back with equal force, nothing necessarily occurring to either.

"Look at you, Matt. Look at your face! A fall, okay. I could see that. *That*. But that - I dunno what to call her - hanging out with you boys all the time, God knows what you think she'll do for you - and bunnies? Sure, fine. I buy all of it, Matt. One-hundred percent."

"Cause it's the truth!"

"But when you come home with a face like yours, with a split lip, how'd that happen? Who tore your clothes? Your arm is practically broken. We're gonna go the emergency room. So, we're going to have to find the money for that now, too. You aren't a tough kid, Matt," she says, and the next part truly confused him. "You *can't* be."

"But those kids, Ma. Those guys," he cries out. "You don't know them. You don't see them like I do. How they treat me and Chucky. How they spit on me everyday. And now. Now you're saying I'm weak, Ma, right? I'm a fucking pussy?"

"No! Matty, no," she goes on to herself. "Lord, it all comes out wrong when it does, right?" She paused; her fingers did this twiddling thing like she was attempting to pull the correct thoughts of the air in front of her head. "You are my son. Mine. And I love you. But we almost lost you once. And we aren't going to lose you again." She tosses her glass back and finishes the drink in one loud swallow. "End of discussion."

He was grounded for two weeks. Seth Michaels, whose knee Matty stomped, wouldn't walk without crutches for another six. He had a terrible dream that night. All he could remember when he woke was the sounds of the train, the snapping of twigs, and the echoing screams of Cat.

Chapter Eleven

"Okay, Gabe. Just a quick pinch and we're all done," Dr. Harwood said. "You won't feel a thing."

Gabriel, only three-and-a-half and wise for his age, could tell better. It was the smell. Something about when the doctor rubbed that cold white swab on his arm. He had woken up not feeling too good and his mommy told him they would Go-to-dockah, and he didn't like the Go-To-Dockah because he promised you that it won't hurt a bit, and he's squirming in Allie's lap like the worm that just got hooked and you could bet your ass he'd be crying in five-four-three-two-one-

"Gabe, come on," Allie said. "Hold still. Please, sweety."

"No."

"Gabe, this will be easier if-"

"No, mommy!" Gabe weezed. "Dokah pinch. Dokah *pinch*!"

"Damnit," she said too loud for her own comfort. "Mommy's not asking now." She wrapped her arms around him in a bear hug until he couldn't wriggle anymore, exhausting him after a few moments. "I think we're good."

"Thanks, Allison," the pediatrician said.

The needle went in and Gabe was right. It *did* hurt.

A lot.

"Please, Matt," Allie said, weeping into the phone. "Just tell me. How much longer are you going to be there? They won't tell me anything over the phone."

"Hon, it's only been a few days," he says.

"But how much longer, Matt?"

She had put their son to bed early. He had forgotten all about the doctor's office by the time they came back from Toys R Us with his new Thomas the Tank Engine rip-off and damn-near played himself to sleep. She had a glass of wine, then another - was going to order from Saigon Palace but decided to call her husband first. "I don't know how much longer I can do this on -" There was a long sigh; he could hear her breathing.

"On your own?" he said into the receiver, the cold metal coil from the payphone felt awkward against his wrist.

Matt could hear the frustration in her voice, the desperation of someone who has no one to turn to when all of the fucks run out. "I don't know, Alison. Honestly. I don't." He started to well up. Could feel the tears coming. *I don't mean to hurt you,* he thinks. *This is not your fault.* "I only see the doc three days a week, and that's usually for dosage adjustments. I meet with my caseworker, but that's usually the same thing everyday. I don't know why I'm still here. It's like they are waiting for me to pass a test that they haven't handed out yet."

"I just don't get it." She pauses. "I just don't know why you would do this to us. To me. Because if you loved-"

"To you? You think I did this to you?" he nearly shouted. Then looked over his shoulder at Mikey, one of the night orderlies sitting behind the glass at the front desk. Mikey was a big guy, probably a Hockey Kid in his younger years, and someone Matt definitely had no intention of pissing off during a phone call.

"Decide to do what you did, yes. To be in there and not with me - with your son - who was sick today, *again*. Another ear infection."

Her words stung, but she wasn't wrong.

Matt rubbed his temples with his thumb and forefinger. "Tubes, did they say?" he asked.

"Not yet. They want to test his hearing first. But who knows?"

"Christ," Matt replied. There was a long pause. Her breathing sounded rushed, like she was silently weeping. "Allie. I hope you know that - I *know* you know that I'm trying, right? That this isn't some kind of vacation for me."

There was a longer pause on her end. He could hear the clink of the glass and realized *Oh, she's finishing the wine.*

"Are you?" she said and took a final swallow. "That's pretty good," and let out a little chuckle that hung in the air before dying.

"Of course, for you," he whisper-shouted. The hospital was not someplace you wanted to have anyone see you upset, and there were always people – Mikey, in this case - around to see if you were getting upset. "And Gabe. For *all* of us, Allie. Why is that not good enough?"

"Matt," Allison said. "I think Gabe just woke up, so I'm going to check on him."

"But -"

But there was only a click.

———

Conway is in the Rec Center. Matt overslept, missed breakfast and the first group of the day. He couldn't settle down after his phone call with Allie, so the night nurse had to give him some Trazodone, which at first didn't seem to do much of anything, but then everything went wishy-washy. He ate a granola bar and some more of that gasoline coffee and went out to find his friend. *Is that what we are?* he thought. Not sure, but for the past week Conway was the most intimate connection he'd had, he realized. And that counted his wife. As he approached the court, he noticed that the old man had a hell of a free-throw.

"Swish," Matt called, surprising Conway, who tripped up, the ball flying past the backboard. "Oh, shit! Sorry, Zach!" Conway turns to him with a collegiate stare.

"Thought you only played chess?"

Matt hustles down to the hoop, passes the ball to his friend. "Well, you know how bad I suck at cards. What's your game?" he asks.

"Don't really have one," Zach replies, shooting again. This one circles the rim twice before sliding down the net. "Just like to shoot. Just me, the net, and the echoes of my younger self delusionally thinking I could take on Dr. J."

Matt collects the ball and passes back to him. He shoots. Matt passes. He scores again.

"I suck, so that's fine," Matt says.

"Are you okay? I didn't see you in group. Or breakfast. Overslept?"

"Something like that," Matt nods. "They had to give me Trazodone."

"Ah," Conway smiles. "The sweet slumber of off-label sedatives. They will knock you on your ass if you're new to the game." His chuckle matches the echoes of the bouncing ball.

Matt takes the ball, dribbles past Zach and jumps,

shoots, and misses the scoreboard by a mile. He lands and immediately puts his hand on his leg, gasps.

"Hey, need any help? Pull something?" Conway asks.

Matt limps to the sideline.

"No. I have a rod in my femur. Accident when I was a kid. Haven't you noticed the limp?" He hikes his shorts up just a bit until the bottom half of his left thigh exposes an ugly canal of flesh.

"Can't say I have, Matt," Conway answers. "Do you want to take five and talk about it?"

"Not really. I mean, not now. I'm good. Just not used to jumping around. Haven't done that since I was in school."

"That's fine," Conway says. "You know where to find me if you want to."

The walk back to the unit is quiet. The men enjoy their company, but also acknowledge the need for distant silence as an attribute.

"Don't know if it's uncouth, Zach. But I gotta ask."

"How long have I been here?" Conway cuts him off. "Well, that's the question of the day."

"It just seems, and I'm sorry to jump out and ask, but it seems like you know everything about this place. I figured since it's the unit for short-termers, you couldn't possibly have been here more than a few weeks, right?"

At this, Zach Conway begins to laugh.

"What? Zach, what's so funny?"

―――

Later that night Matt is reading in the television room. He hears the night orderly, Barry, coming down the hall, the echoes of his oversize keychain reflecting off the tiles. "Checks," he says, banging on the bathroom door. A muffled sound can be heard and Barry repeats   "Checks," only this time louder. "Second time. Need to see your hands and face!"

This was true. Matt got into the swing of things early on, always a quick adapter. But for the new patients? Especially ones who haven't the opportunity to stay at a psych ward? This was new to them, scary. And the last thing you think you would want to do with a new - possibly agitated - patient is to provide more disruption and chaos where it seems no more could possibly fit. But them's the bricks.

The door opens.

"- the fuck, man. I'm taking a shower!" said a young woman. "This is ridiculous."

"Regulations."

"Regulations mean I gotta show my ass, too?"

The door slammed.

Barry turned his attention to Matt.

"Checks," he says. Matt nodded silently. As he walked away, Matt began to focus on Barry's moves, his pace. He was amazed that he had thought him overweight. Seeing him now, not in a dream, the guy couldn't be more than a buck seventy-five. It's funny how the mind plays tricks on you. Really funny.

———

The summer was going to be tough. Matt could just tell. School had just ended for the year and he wasn't happy about it. Everything seemed sour. Chucky was going to be in summer school to make up for the chemistry class he failed; Billy's aunt rented a cottage up on Lake Chocorua for them to stay until August. Which left Cat - which was good - Matt loved hanging out with Cat, but Chucky was his best friend. Cat was his best friend's sister. And it felt kind of - how did it feel? He didn't know. If Chucky or Billy heard him say it, they would rash on him forever but - he guessed she felt like home. But Cat also had sailing lessons out on the pond twice a week. So yes, it was summer. But for the first time in a long time, Matt wasn't too excited about it. Sure, he could spend some extra time trying to master the combos in *Tekken* or maybe try to get the SHOWTIME multi-ball in Addams Family pinball at House of Pizza. Maybe he would hang out at the fort. He didn't know. The bridge? *Not safe to go alone,* he thought. *Especially after last time. That cat.* You assholes. *None of us will go down there now. That was* our *place. Billy mentioned it once in passing and Cat nearly collapsed from post-traumatic stress.*

"And those posters," he heard himself say out loud.

Lydia Harrington had plastered the better part of every telephone pole in the tri-city area with Kinko's copies showing a grainy photo of Mr. Brown in grey-scale simply stating-

BOYS, BROKEN

LOST:
Mr. Brown
Not Shy
Small Reward If Found

Matt's heart broke to know that no, Mrs. Harrington, you were never going to find that cat, and you really did not want to have him returned. Poor lady didn't even remember to leave a call back number on the poster.

He was walking down Cedar Street when the thunderheads opened and the rain began to spit out onto the hot pavement, releasing that sweet aroma that Matt could easily list in his All-Time Top Five. He cut across onto Jackson Street and across to Walnut Hill. It wasn't pouring yet, but the trek had soaked through his tee. He decided the fort would be the best course of action. To seek shelter.

It started coming down harder as he made his way up the hill, but the leaves provided some cover on his way to the bus. Inside, Matt thumbed through an assortment of DC comics from a milk crate they found behind a convenience store on Pine Street. He chose his favorite graphic novel - "The Death of Superman" - and began to read. Outside, the rain evolved into a downpour. *I was right,* Matt thought. *This summer is going to suck.*

Danny Johnson was having a fine summer break. His arm had healed up from last year, and though not at full capacity, he had thrown a solid season with the Sox. They came in first, of course. They always came in first and what Danny couldn't accomplish with pitching, PJ and Corey made up for in walk-offs. Nearly every single time Corey stepped up to the plate, his swing sent him to third or home. PJ was a solid contact hitter. If it were about ten years later, one might compare him to a young Dustin Pedroia. Seth wasn't able to play due to his torn ACL (the Sox had blamed the incident to just kids being kids and Seth taking a bad tackle in touch football down at Vet's field), but he still suited up, which pleased Danny fine. You always support your team.

He was excited that they were going to be freshmen, joining Tony Quinn and the Hill brothers at Reedy Memorial. It occurred to him that those other kids, those wastes of space, would also be tagging along for the next four years, and that didn't sit well with him at all. Asshole kids in the wrong place at the wrong time. And that girl? Well, she still had one more year in middle school. *And maybe she's a dyke*, he thought. But if she wasn't, he could tell that she would be a good contender for the "Spit or Swallow" game, though even he wasn't quite sure of the details. He only knew that slut girls did it, and if there was any girl he knew that had the potential to be a slut, it was a girl who goes off in the woods with boys all day, and one of them her brother - could you just puke? *And that gimp,* he thought. *Don't forget him. Almost cost you your pitching arm. Almost got you in trouble with that leaking duffle bag.* But he knew that they wouldn't be a problem for too long. Those kids were nothing compared to Danny and his friends. Nothing.

As he approached Walnut Hill, the rain picked up, the crack of thunder caught him off guard. It was warm so he wasn't wearing a jacket and the potential downpour made Danny uneasy. He saw a glimmer in the woods. *The fuck is that*, he thought. He cut through the Scolaro's backyard and hopped the fence, making his way towards the twinkling light. Then he saw what he was looking at. All of a sudden, he had an idea and smiled. Yes. He knew it was going to be a great summer.

During the storm, Matt dreamt, but that might not be the right word. It was more a series of images he couldn't necessarily connect. The milk truck. His mother's wheelchair abandoned in the backyard. A train rumbling down the tracks. Coffee cups. Fire. Punches being thrown. Thunder crashing. Pizza. A baby crying. A cat screeching. People shouting. Shouting. Shouting. Screaming. SCREAMING SCREAMING -

He woke to the sound of thunder, the raindrops gunning off the rooftop like pebbles in a blender. His face was covered in mist; the curtains that Cat had installed may have looked nice but did absolute fuck-all to shelter from the elements.

The first rock hit him before he had time to think. Matt had just opened the bus door when a finger-sized piece of shale zipped him in the shoulder.

"Arrr!" he gasped.

The second goes wide, hits the bus with a *ping*, and ricochets into the dirt. Another connects with Matt's knee, his right, and a fourth knicks the top of his left ear. Fresh blood poured onto his crew cut, warm and sticky. Chaos was everywhere. Everything slowed down and he had to think think think!

What is going on? I'm being attacked. Attacked. Attacked.

His eyes were wide when he finally noticed Danny and Corey just outside of the bushes. They were the ones.

"So, this is your new place, huh, Gimp?" Danny wound up for another throw, but Matt charged him. Neither Corey nor Danny were expecting this move, so they weren't prepared for when Matt connected, sending him into Corey, and the three of them down the hill. The boys rolled over rocks and moss for about twenty feet. Corey dug his boots into the ground to stop, but Danny wasn't as lucky, and rolled into the side of an elm stump ribs-first.

"Ah, geesh!" Danny groaned, holding his side.

Corey stood, grabbed a large stick and ran to where Matt's pile of a body was slumped on the ground.

Matt didn't move. He was in an immense amount of pain, might even have a cracked rib. But he knew he had to play possum. They already had attacked him with rocks, which could have been deadly. If they caught him breathing, who knew what would happen?

Corey wound up to hit him, but then Danny said, "No." He forced himself to his feet. "We know where they are now. We *know*. Come on."

With that, they were off, and Matt knew that for the foreseeable future, summer was going to be a shitshow.

That night Matthew Rode lay awake staring out the window; from his perspective he saw the lampposts upside down. He noticed the peculiar way the screen was on the inside of the glass, and suddenly realized why - to protect the patients from smashing the windows and hurting themselves. This brought on more peculiar thoughts of the other peculiar things he had noticed about Knott's Haven's design. There were no edges on anything. This wasn't just on rounded corners or door frames, which, though unusual aren't necessarily out of the ordinary. No, there were no edges or corners on *anything*. The tables were round with belt-sanded formica tops; the shower curtains didn't begin or end - just continued on an unending loop from inside the wall with no rod to hang it from; the sink had no faucet but an arcing jet of water that angled out at a tepid temperature when you waved your hand in front of an infrared sensor; there was no lever on the toilet, just a bowl that somehow knew when you were done; he thought of these things, all of these things that in any other situation could find himself saying that he understood why you would need to protect those types from themselves. He could certainly rationalize *that*. The last thing you wanted was a bunch of patients breaking glass for a quick throat stab or eye gouge, or to tie some poor nurse to a shower curtain rod, opening her blouse as he muffled her screams with a sharp piece of window pressed delicately against her throat. If she was wearing a skirt he may need to slip his hand up her thigh to see if she was ready for him as she screamed; to move on, to fill a few socks with rolls of quarters the assistants kept in the nursing station for the vending machines, to go to town on the one male overnight orderly - Barry - late fifties, introduced himself to Matt by pulling out his cellphone and showing him pictures of his daughter, Colleen, just got a full ride to Colby College; Barry, at least thirty pounds overweight so if the beating didn't kill him, it may certainly trigger the coronary his primary care in Stoneham kept warning him about.

Matt thinks of his wife and how they met at a coin-op laundry his fifth year at State, how he forgot to remove a ballpoint pen from his jeans pocket, how it fell into the dryer and how it painted her week's dirties a royal blue; how she had shouted at him until they laughed, how they went home that night, how they went to bed; he thinks of his son, Gabriel, and how they would play robots in the living room or "wee-ball" in the backyard, or hoisting him onto his shoulders as they perused through the North End for the Feast of Saint Anthony; he thought of Allie on their wedding night, too loaded to get out of her dress and falling asleep in his arms, how all they wanted to do was be partners in crime - he thinks of these things as the moon looks at him, as it had looked down at many a hopeless man, as it had the night some twenty years ago when his friends finally decided to act. It wasn't the depravity of any of these thoughts that terrifies him, no. It was the rationalizing. One thought comes to his mind then, and he won't sleep tonight. No.

What if they're right, he thinks.
What if I am crazy?

Part Three:

Cold as Ice

Chapter Twelve

Billy shows up to the bus with two things. The first is a cold extra-cheese pizza from Sal's on Center Street. The second was a fresh black eye. Though the kids knew it was from his father during one of his "Miller High Life Champagne-Of-Beers-I'll-show-you's", they would never have brought it up to him. Every family has their stories - the Thanksgiving dinners ruined by an uncle putting out his Pall Mall in the gravy, the sister who got pregnant from a kid from the city and sent to live with her aunt in Vermont until the baby was born. Kids knew better then to talk about that shit. Especially when it was one of your friends. One of *yours*.

Billy placed the pizza on the driver's seat, took a slice, and proceeded to the end of the bus. He opened the emergency door and squat down on his haunches, awkwardly trying to sit without dropping his slice onto the floor (bad) or the dirt (worse). His face throbbed with every bite he took, but the pizza tasted fantastic.

Everyone takes a slice and eats.

"So, what are we going to do?" Cat asked Matt. The sun had started to set over the trees, creating a beautiful starburst of orange-purple. Nickie was resting next to Chucky, and it appeared to Matt at least, that he was suspiciously close to putting his arm around her shoulder.

"About what?" Matt answered. Though his face was scabbed up, his arms and legs covered in scratches and bruises from his roly-poly down the hill, he was dead serious. "This summer? Danny and those dicks? You and me?"

He stopped.

"What do you mean?" Cat said, and then "Oh."

Matt kept thinking about that nightmare he had, how he couldn't forget the screaming. And when he wasn't ruminating on that, he had been coming up with a series of plans to deal with the summer. They would be a man down, since Billy would be with his aunt in New Hampshire.

"I don't know what we'll do. Chucky's not around. Neither are you."

"Only a few days," she said. "Just a few."

A young teen will act as if every single aspect of his life is the most important thing that's ever occurred in history, in a kind of hyper-realistic way. But isn't that because, at the time, it is? The tragedy is that it's true.

Matt continues.

"I figure I'm dodging bullets most of the summer. Can't run, right? And the only safe place besides my bed is here. Was here." His voice trails off as he remembers that he hadn't told the group that the boys knew where the bus was. Cat and Chucky probably guessed Matt was jumped on the way home from school. Technically they wouldn't be wrong.

Matt looks off over the sky as the purples and oranges fade into the horizon over a town starting to go to sleep. Cat touches his face. He looks at her.

"Promise me," she begins. The crescent moon is emerging, and she takes his hand, still aching from how he landed on it during the fall. "Promise me you'll be safe. That when we aren't here you won't do something stupid. That no matter what, you make sure you think of me, of us. That you run, Matt. You run if you need to."

"I pro-" he begins, but before he could say it, she had pulled him close and kissed him with soft, sweet lips that tasted of cherry chapstick. This was his first. He didn't know what to do with his hands, so he awkwardly ran a hand softly through her fire-hair, and when they had pulled away, he could see her eyes were watering. She leans her head on his shoulder as crickets begin to sing their night song. After a while, they sleep.

BOYS, BROKEN

Matthew wakes in a cold sweat. He could have sworn he smelled smoke, burning twigs, the ashen taste of bark embers. But lying on the cold, naked mattress on the unit with its reflective white tiled walls he remembers and almost chokes up. *That's right,* he thinks. *I'm still here. Still.*

A scream comes from somewhere, reflections bouncing off the walls in the hall like zigzag dynamite, finding its intended target (Matthew's ears) and immediately triggering a migraine so intense that the nausea feels like an afterthought. Sleep was his last resort, but it didn't look like he would get anymore tonight.

Chapter Thirteen

The morning was a ghost. Still awake with a throbbing head and red swollen eyes, Matthew took his black coffee back to his room and sat on the plastic mattress, squinting as the sunbeams splayed through the window panes and permeated into his brain. He could hear his heartbeat throbbing, pulsating a one-and-a-two quarter-note swingtime. Nice beat, he thought, but can you dance to it?

Outside he saw the day staff pulling up in their Volvos and Subarus, coming from homes where they could sleep at night next to their husbands and wives, kiss their sons and daughters goodnight, and send them off to school in the morning. It's summertime, you idiot, he thought. No school for now. Yes, he agreed in thought. But he hated them. Hated them so much for their freedom. Hated them for their lives. Wished the roles were reversed. Wished.

Conway wasn't around. For the rest of the day, Matthew noodled on the piano but mostly stayed in his room. He didn't eat much. It seemed he lost his appetite, or, like the social-smoker that would always bum his Winstons outside of Matt's regular bar on Fridays, only really wanted to eat when others were around. He thought back to his first semester of college and how his Freshman Fifteen was closer to twentyone.

BOYS, BROKEN

The rain begins to pour in sheets as thunder and lightning boom over the quiet middle-New England hamlet.

Cat knows something is wrong the second she wakes up. She hears the thump-thump-thump of either walls being punched, or books being thrown. Either way, whatever noise had stirred her from her sleep, it wasn't good. Not in her house, no. Noise meant trouble.

"...the hell said it was okay, huh?"

Even coming through the walls, muffled and bassy, she could tell her folks were at it, and by the sound, her father was winning the fight.

"I can't fucking believe it!" he said, the yell sounding shrill and unusual, not the ruffled voice of the father she knew.

"Please!"

"Please? Fuck you! Or did he do that enough last night?"

Cat was confused. She knew her parents fought. Everybody fights, she wasn't naive. But she couldn't understand what was going on and it scared her, a rumbling nervous tickle in her stomach. She needed to pee.

There was a CRASH and then she heard her mother cry out, and then heard Chucky shout "No no NO!"

Not knowing what to do and with no clue as to what she was doing, Cat opened her door, and saw to her horror that her father was on top of her mother, his hands around her throat. She suddenly understood that the crash she heard was from the China hutch, which it appears to have been knocked over by her father, dishes crashing and shattering like so many cymbals. Her brother was balled on the couch, bleeding from his mouth.

"My brother," her father said. "My fucking brother? You whore!"

At this Cat became terrified. What was that word, and who was this monster that had replaced her daddy?

"Daddy, what are you - "she began.

He stayed on top of her mother, his arms atop hers, pinning her to the ground as she wriggled like a worm trying to escape the hook, but can't, because it's a worm. Without missing a beat, without glancing up, he said "Go back to bed, sweety. Mommy and daddy are having a little argument, that's all."

She looked in her mother's eyes, and gasped as she saw that the left was bruised shut, both dripping with tears. It was an awful, panicked look that hurt her. How could he be doing this? Whatever happened, could it be that bad? Her father had never, for all she knew, laid a hand on anyone. He was her gentle Daddy, a big dopey bear that would rub his whiskers against her cheek as he kissed her goodnight. This thing in the living room, amongst the broken collectible plates adorned by the faces of JFK and Jesus, this couldn't be her father.

She heard sniffling from across the room and realized that she had forgotten that Chucky was still there. Her brother was bigger then she was, muscular, and was pretty good at throwing a punch or two, as she had seen down by the tracks against those Sox. But here, crumpled in a mess on the couch, he seemed more scared than she was.

From the kitchen the phone began to ring.

A few hours before Jack Dawson had cold-cocked his wife, Vic Shaw, the drunk that was Billy's father had gotten into a bit of a pickle. With the rain coming down as hard as it was, and with Billy gone for the summer, Vic had no one to help reshingle the roof over his kitchen a few blocks over. The old house was already full of termites and rot and Vic would be goddamned if he was going to pay for exterminators. So, for the past few days, he had come home from work, pulled the 12-foot ladder out of the garage, and went to work during the calming summer nights, hammering and shingling and hammering.

BOYS, BROKEN

The night of the storm he had seen the thunderheads on his way home from work but thought that they would pass. August is a better time for big storms, he thought. And like the nights before, he took his Husky toolbox and his recoilless hammer and went to work. Tonight, though, it being a Friday and all, he had also brought a pint of Johnnie Red, and by 10:00 PM or so, with most of the burn down his throat he decided it was time to stop hammering. He closed his eyes and fell asleep.

What woke Vic Shaw was just around the time Cat had opened her bedroom door to witness the hostage situation in her living room. The roof, splintered and creaking under the weight of wet, soggy Vic, finally decided to give way, sending him careening through one story of poor Yankee craftsmanship, exploding through his solid walnut butcher-block kitchen island (*good* Yankee craftsmanship). He was hurting like a sonofabitch. His kitchen was full of weather and debris.

He picked up the phone and was about to call 911 but then quickly put the phone back on the receiver. *What kind of an idiot are you*, he thought. *You'll be the laughing stock of the whole town if the police find out about this.*

So, he did the next best thing. He called one of his drinking buddies from Tab's Pub, Jack Dawson. He knew that Billy hung around with his kids, so maybe he could come and help or something. He picked up the phone again. *Now*, he thought, *if I can only remember his number.*

Cat noticed the clock on the stove said it was 2:37 AM. No one should be calling at this time. What she didn't know, what none of them knew, was that on the other end was the decrepit waste that sent Billy to the Lake's region for the summer. Unaware of this fact, and desperate for some semblance of help, she darted for the kitchen. Her father wasn't pleased by this course of action, leaping to his feet in chase. Cat's hand grabbed the receiver and before it was even next her mouth, shouted "Help! Help!" into it before being grabbed by gorilla arms around her waist, and being thrown across the kitchen, her left side slamming into the squeaky door of the Kenmore refrigerator. It made a guttural, awful sound the way you'd think that nightmares would sing if they could. Jack bent to pick up the receiver and-

"Ga...naaah," was the only sound he could utter. He dropped to one knee, and then to his side, the receiver bouncing off the tobacco stained wallpaper like some broken half-pendulum.

What Cat couldn't see at first, the stars in her eyes clouding her field of vision, was that Chucky had driven 6 inches of his father's Husky flathead screwdriver down into his shoulder. She didn't even know where he came from. There wasn't much blood. Moaning, but that was all. Chucky seemed to bounce on his feet. He looked at his sister, then simply mouthed *I'm sorry* before running to his room with a bang that could have been the door slamming shut or the thunder outside.

Neither would surprise her.

The room had become loud with silence now, minus the wriggling scrapes of Jack Dawson's legs as they splayed back and forth across the linoleum tile. For a single bizarre moment, Cat wondered how hard she would need to scrub with the Dr. Bronner's her mother kept under the sink - the soap that smelled like peppermint and castile – if she were ever able to lift the spots of her father's blood from the grout work. Across the hall in the parlor, her mother finally found her voice and screamed.

It took seven minutes for the ambulance to show up, and another fifteen for Mrs. Dawson to convince the EMTs that she would drive Jack to the ER herself. Twenty minutes later, as Cat drifted in and out, her last thought just of confusion about what had happened, she lay in her bed (avoiding her left side), knowing that deep down Chucky had to do what he did. She also was certain that her brother probably had snuck out the window and was currently sleeping at the fort, or was on the run, and that scared her. She was alone now. Alone with the thunder. It was her birthday.

———

Outside in the rain, Chucky ran and ran and ran until his breathing was hard and his spit tasted alkaline. The soaked dirty laces of his Airwalks slapped back and forth against his shins, making a *spuck-spuck* sound, his feet hopelessly drenched from the storm; he could feel the big toe of his left foot breaking through his worn sock. His mind raced with questions he didn't think he wanted the answers to. What had he done? How did it get so bad tonight? Why did his dad transform so suddenly into a monster he'd never seen before, snapping like a branch with no more bend you keep hanging from, farther and farther, until there's no other way to go but break?

"Damn him," he thought. "This is all his fault. Him and his freaking booze. All of the time with the drinking." And while true, the child didn't necessarily know if what Chucky had done would constitute self-defense or not. Shit, he had stabbed his own father. Could have killed him. And suppose he did? He knew he hadn't, of course, his mother was probably at that very moment pressing a dishtowel to plug up the wound, and worse, apologizing. But again, he thought, what if he did. What if his father were dead? Say goodbye to all his friends, his videogames, his school. Goodbye to summer vacation, baseball and water guns. Say ta-ta to swimming down in the lake, rope swings and fishing. Instead, he would probably get locked up, either in juvie or one of those residential houses run by the state out Metrowest, places where orphans and runaways are stored. Or maybe be committed to one of those youth mental institutions on the Northshore. Places of neglect and filth and dark ignored pain. Chucky wouldn't last a week in one of those places, no. And what about Cat? Would he dare risk the thought of her alone, her brother cast aside with the rest of the lunatic fringe?

No, of course not. His father could go crawl in a ditch somewhere, but Cat? She was everything to him.

With all these thoughts in his head, he didn't notice his sprint had turned to a trot, and now he had come full-stop at the base of Mapleway. He bent at the waist and tried to catch his breath. He could be a fast kid when needed, but he wasn't a trained runner and the stitch up his side would be a reminder for the next day or so. The crack of thunder sounded like Wade Boggs slugging one out of Fenway, and he realized he should probably get out from under the giant trees, but really, the way Mapleway curved and grew, the street was covered by a canopy of cascading branches. It was virtually impossible to avoid the trees.

He was soaked, his shirt sticking to his chest, his Wranglers cold and heavy. There was nothing worse than wet blue jeans, he thought. Took forever to dry. He needed shelter and soon. He kept thinking of how his mother always warned him to dress for rain or he'd be sure to catch his death. Could you believe it? He could almost laugh.

He didn't want to go towards town, not after tonight. It was late and he knew there would be a chance he would be stopped by a patrolman if he was discovered. And then he would want to know what a kid was up to at 2:00 AM in the rain, no coat, did your parents know what you were doing? Worse, he would bring him home in the patrol car, and he knew that his parents, if they were home by the ER by that time, would certainly send him back to the ER if he came home in the back of a squad car.

Also, worse, he knew, was that he had broken the family code. Well, the *unspoken* code, really. The Dawsons were an Irish family so proud, that his father graced Slainte at each meal. Before every dinner, Jack drank a six of Highlife, alone, followed by at least a shot of Dewars. He would then eat his supper, also alone, and then order the rest of the family in. There, he would make sure his family ate until they were sated. But they had to eat what they took, and if a plate wasn't cleaned, well. It wasn't out of the ordinary for Jack Dawson to unleash a backhand or two on his son, a closed fist on his wife. He was the breadwinner. If he didn't keep his family in line, who would? And to think that the Dawsons were an outlier would have been sheer ignorance. Most of the kids in school would show up with mystery bruises or cuts from time-to-time. But, like most Irish Catholic families, you simply did not talk about what went on behind closed doors. A family's business was theirs. And to hell with anyone who made it their own.

He didn't want to go to the Shire. The climb would have been a death sentence and with the ground so wet, he was liable to slip on some moss and break his neck careening down the hillside only to be found by a family of raccoons who wouldn't know what to make of such a sight.

No. There had to be somewhere else.

There was a sound behind him. Breathing maybe. A crass, raspy noise coming from just beyond the trees. He could smell a scent beyond the rain on the cement, an odor that was particularly surprising at this time of night. It smelled like the aftershave his father kept in the medicine cabinet that he would splash on his cheeks the days he felt like erasing his stubble. It was an oaken, musky smell; something worn by a gentleman on a night out or-

There was another noise. This one sounded higher, breathy, and definitely not that of a man. He turned slowly, the laces of his sneakers slithering in the muddy puddles like worms and discovered the cause of the alien noises. There, not twenty feet in front of him, at the end of the Eustis Court dead end, precariously close to the thicket where his sister was attacked earlier in the season, was a silver Grand Marquis. Or was it a Crown Vic? Chucky could never tell them apart. When you got down to it, minus the trooper usually sitting driver, the Crown Victoria and Grand Marquis were basically couches on wheels. He remembered his father telling him they were the most comfortable cruising vehicle one could drive, minus getting both-miles-to-the-gallon.

At first, he couldn't tell exactly what it was they were doing, the windows fogged up, streaks of handprints on the windows. But as

he inched closer, he could clearly see the bobbing up and down of a head in between the legs of the other person. He didn't know what it was by name, but by sight he could theorize that this action was the one the guys at school spoke about in whispers at the bus stop and locker room. He knew what sex was – he wasn't ignorant. He had seen plenty from the old porno mags strewn around the bridge, leftover fantasies from other teenagers too embarrassed to spank it in the privacy of their own bedrooms or showers - but this was the nineties, long before broadband and instant access anything. He had never actually seen a blowjob. Hell, Chucky's family couldn't even afford a personal computer, let alone the internet. Matt was always tossing those "Free 30 Hours of AOL" CD-ROMs into the trash.

"Did you hear something?" The girl's voice came from inside the car, muffled by the rain on the windows that sounded like popcorn.

"What? No, no babe. It's nothing. Don't stop," the other voice answered. "Just the rain -"

"Just the rain? Fuck it was, Kevin! I *heard* something. Out there!"

Chucky froze. He heard more noises, caught a glimpse of the girl's bra. But then she was covered by the silhouette of Kevin as he sat up, started dressing.

"I knew this was a bad idea," the girl said.

He wanted to run. But he didn't, not yet. He slipped into the bushes and waited. He had no idea who this Kevin was, but assumed he would kick his ass if he caught Chucky peeping. But still, he stayed, standing in the rain, listening to the embarrassed sounds of car sex.

The door opened and a pair of big legs stepped out. Kevin was about six feet tall, wore a pair of 501s and a faux-leather jacket he had slipped on over his shirtless chest. He looked familiar, and then it suddenly came to Chucky. Kevin was really Detective Kevin Johnson, Danny's father. With the door open, he also noticed the girl. Only she wasn't a girl. The woman was middle-aged, but you couldn't necessarily tell by the looks of her. She was what the boys in ten or so years would refer to as a MILF or a cougar. She was balled up in the back seat in a black lace bra, and for a split excited second he noticed she wasn't wearing any panties. He saw her entire sex, her red pubic hair shaved up the sides into a landing strip. He could see *everything,* which made him feel engorged and ashamed all at once. Worse, Chucky had also recognized her. She was Gus's wife, Tabitha. Tabby worked at Sammy's Diner part-time as the accountant and also baked the chocolate chip and peanut butter cookies served daily. She was always nice to the neighborhood men, but yikes. He never would have imagined anyone being this nice. *Holy shit,* he thought. *The dude's wife is fucking a cop.*

Officer Johnson called out to the trees and shrubs but Chucky didn't dare make a peep. He was petrified now. He just wanted them to get back in the car and leave. Or at least make enough noise so they couldn't hear him as he fled. But Kevin Johnson didn't turn around. Instead, he went into the bushes about seven feet from Chucky, unbuttoned his Levis, and pissed into the bushes. The rain had died to a spittle and Chucky could hear as the urine plop-plopped against the leaves. It was an embarrassing sound, listening to someone else pee.

After a few endless seconds, the cop finished, buttoned up, and returned to the car. Only this time, he got in the front seat. The car started and Chucky never felt better than he did when he saw it drive away.

Chucky's parents didn't send him to the hospital when he got home. No, they were still absent, and by 10:30 the next morning, when he heard the front door creak open as he lay splayed on the couch, and felt the heavy-thudded footsteps as his father walked in the front door, his body tensed and his bladder filled with hot water. He knew he was dead. But when he saw as both parents sauntered right past him and up the stairs towards their room, he didn't feel relief, which scared him most of all. They looked as pale and tired as ghosts. Purgatory souls.

Chapter Fourteen

The new school year started and Chucky and Matt were in separate classes for the first time since the end of fourth grade. On three different occasions, Chucky wanted to tell Matt what he had seen on the night of the incident out in the woods, but always chickened out. It wasn't that he was nervous about how Matt would react. He was more nervous about what would happen if anyone else found out, especially Danny. He had seen Danny at Sammy's Diner multiple times since he saw his father's cock in the owner's wife. And he knew, just knew, that if it found its way back to him, as things always seemed to do in this town, that Chucky, Cat, hell, maybe even Matt and Billy. They'd all be goners.

Christmas came, and with it Matt got a new Bauer hockey stick. He never skated since the accident, his limp always getting in the way. But he was damn good on a cul-de-sac. Billy, who basically wore a pair of skates from November until April, would teach Matt how to shoot, the puck lifting off the ground like a mini UFO. And though he preferred the warmth of baseball season, he did have to admit that hockey was a fun way to kill the long, brutally dull New England winters, the endless Sunday afternoons that brought nothing but bitter cold and intense sunlight reflecting off snowbanks. The feel of that stick with brand new tape all the way up the handle was one of the best memories he had. The sound of air collapsing in out itself when you made a perfect slap shot. He preferred baseball, but hockey did have its pluses.

It was a cold February day when it happened. "An accident, of course," Coach had said. "Had to have been an accident." But that wasn't the way any of Matt's friends saw it. How Matt saw it.

Billy had made varsity at tryouts and impressed Coach Doyle so much that he put him on as a starter. Right wing. He was a beast in front of the net, battling juniors and seniors twice his size. Varsity practiced double sessions at the rink three days a week, Monday, Wednesday, Thursday. First session was at the ungodly hour of 5:30 AM, which meant he had to be up by 4:30 if he wanted to eat, dress, and walk to school on time - it would be a cold day in hell before Vic Shaw drove his son to practice, that was for damn sure - followed by after-school practice from 2:30 until 5:00. After that, the Junior Varsity team took the ice. They had the luck of only having to practice after school, but then again, they also sucked. Reading and Stoneham would wipe the floor with them most games. No one cared about J.V.

It was a Wednesday practice after school when it occurred. Doyle had just wrapped up with his post-practice, pre-game speech about rah-rah go out and get 'em and such, and ducked outside for a butt, as was his usual routine. Maybe he'd take a pull from his quart of Stoli he kept in the inner pocket of his peacoat. Billy had just come off of a great scrimmage - scored a goal, had even checked PJ Armstrong into the boards.

"Easy, Cam Neely," someone had shouted from the stands, and when Billy looked up, wasn't surprised to see Cat. She'd come by sometimes with her camera when she was bored. She took a snapshot of the smiling boy.

It was practice, it was fun.

He pushed off the boards and began skating backwards, his hips doing a vibrant back-and-forth as he made it to center ice. Overall, he was having a good time. Armstrong, however, being a full year older and three inches taller than Billy, hadn't shared his enthusiasm.

"You fucking serious, numb nuts?" PJ said as he pushed himself to his feet. He spun, kicked off the boards and sailed into Billy at what felt like sixty-an-hour, and grabbed him by his jersey. "Faggots like you, right? It's always you fucking guys." The warm breath in the cold rink pulsed out of PJ's nostrils like dragon smoke. Without flinching, he suckerpunched Billy with his left fist, directly up into his solar plexus, dropping Billy to his knees in a heaving pile of pads. "Get up, asshole! You fucking chicken shit." Some of the older teammates circled around and were laughing at the mess at PJ's feet.

Where was the coach, Billy thought. This was about to go from bad to really fucking bad. He rolled to his side and got to his knees, and that was when PJ spat directly into Billy's mask, the green phlegm freezing instantly as it dripped down his facemask in chunky rivulets. Now he couldn't see, which seemed worse than the beating.

Billy took off his helmet.

"What the hell, man?" he shouted to PJ. "Can't take a hit from a freshman?" He instantly regretted saying that out loud because it appeared that, why yes, PJ couldn't *stand* getting hit by a freshman, but he certainly knew how to *hit a fucking freshman*. PJ took off his helmet and suddenly, to Billy's surprise, seemed to grow even taller as he skated up to his face. His breath smelled like stale Doritos, Billy noticed. "What the hell's your problem, PJ?"

"My problem is fucking punks like you who don't know their role. Haven't earned shit," he said. His friends cheered. "You come here, a fucking freshman, and think you can get on *my* team? Play with *my* friends? On *my* ice?" He pushed Billy hard. He skidded back and tried to T-stop with his skates but went ass-over-teakettle and sat down hard. It hurt. PJ inched closer and reached down, extending his hand.

"Sorry about that," he said. "Guess I got out of control." Billy reached up and PJ pulled him up with a yank so hard, Billy heard his elbow pop out of its socket. Billy screamed.

"Hey, man!" It was Tyler Nelson. He was a junior, and a well-liked member of the team. "PJ, I think he's hurt. Quit it and get to the showers. Now!"

He turned to Tyler.

"Oh, he's just being fucking dramatic, man," he said as he turned to Billy. "Right, you faggot?"

He still held Billy by the wrist; tears streaming down Billy's cheeks. Slowly, he nodded his head, but his eyes clearly said *Help Me*.

But instead of kicking PJ's ass, or punching him in the face, or hell, even getting the attention of Coach Doyle – *where the hell is coach* - Tyler repeated himself.

"Armstrong, we're going to hit the showers. All of us," he stared at the teammates who had circled around, their laughing stopped, smiles beginning to fade. "We're all going to the locker room. And if I don't see you there by the time my skates are off," he pushed PJ's shoulder. "Then I'm coming back for you."

And for a second, Billy thought, *What? Is that it?* But Nelson had spoken his piece and was off the ice before Billy knew what was happening. Standing alone, the cold air separating the two boys by only inches, PJ released Billy from his grasp. Billy coughed a little, his chest still hurt from the punch. He felt like he was going to puke. He bent over to grab his helmet, and that was when PJ turned. He grabbed the leaning Billy by his jersey, one hand on his neck, the other by the seat of his pants, and hurled him head first into the boards. The rink was so quiet that PJ could hear the audible POP as the C-1 vertebrae in Billy's neck crushed on impact.

Billy collapsed onto his chest, his body bent on the ice in an ugly L-position, a ball of clothes and flesh. PJ stood over the helpless kid, could hear as the breathing slowed, snot and bloody drool dripping from his face, inching its way across the cold ice like a snail.

BOYS, BROKEN

PJ heard a sound and looked. Cat Dawson, who had been sitting on the bleachers, a binder notebook open on her lap, had dropped her pen. She was visibly shaking.

"Wh-wh-what did you-" and she trailed off. Something in her mind said *camera*. Immediately, her hands were at her backpack, fumbling with the zipper. She found her Kodak and *CLICK*. She wanted to yell, scream for help, but all she did was take pictures, her index finger pressing on the camera's trigger - CLICK - CLICK - CLICK - until there was no film left.

And the whole time, PJ didn't move. He didn't flinch. He didn't run. Once the room was silent, save for the buzz of the arena fluorescents overhead, PJ skated off of the ice to meet his teammates in the locker room. His eyes met the girl's. He smirked, and then walked away.

Coach Doyle returned from his smoke break ten minutes later, and by this time, hadn't even looked over at the ice. He was heading towards the locker room as the JV team was heading out. It was then that he heard Brandon Ditallio, Captain of the JV squad shout, "Holy shit! Coach, Coach!" Doyle headed towards the shouts from the JV squad.

"Jesus, Mary and Joseph," he shouted. He looked in the direction of the ice and bolted, all the while screaming, *"Call 911! Somebody, call 911!"*

He didn't just jump the boards so much as vault them, and, running out onto the ice, slid on his side next to Billy like he was Trot Nixon beating a throw to home. "Come on, guy," he said, rubbing his back gently, and then panicked. All at once he remembered the long hours of CPR training and first aid he had to log in order to get certified; how could he have forgotten the first rule of someone with a possible spinal injury is to *never move the fucking body?*

Many of the squad had crowded the ice, some of the varsity crew out now, hearing the commotion and panic. "Don't do this, Damnit," the coach screamed like he was giving an order. "Do not fucking do this!" He looked up at some of the faces, at PJ. "Has anyone called the - will somebody please just call the fucking cops? Help me, here, damnit!"

But it was too late.

His face was an ashen grey, his eyes an ugly cross. Blood had pooled from his ears and nose, as thick and mucousy as jelly freezing on the ice. There was no movement from his chest, no crying, no pleading. Just the empty silence of air and ice. By the time the paramedics arrived, there just wasn't enough time. He was three weeks from his fifteenth birthday.

―――

Marcia Rode didn't know what to do. She put the phone down and a feeling of great unease settled all around her. Linda Dawson had just phoned with the report. "Some kind of freak accident," she had told her. "During practice. Jesus."

Marcia had only met Billy a few times, knew that he was a constant sidekick to Chucky when they all hung around together. He was a big kid, but quiet. Gentle, perhaps. When she first found out that he was teaching her son hockey, she thought Matt had been joking. Why would such a nice boy be playing such a violent sport? And just look at where it led, she figured.

"Did you tell the kids?" Marcia asked.

"Tell them? Well, no."

"No?" Marcia repeated, surprising herself with how shocked she seemed.

"Well, what would I say? Marcia, those kids, they are all they've got. How do I look my Chucky in the face and tell him that one of his best friends is- I mean, listen to me. I can't even say it to you. It's just not real."

BOYS, BROKEN

Marcia poured a finger of gin into her glass and downed it in a slow gulp. Linda was right. How would she tell Matt? How does anyone tell their kid that their friend has died? *Jesus*, she thought.

"They're only kids," Linda whispered into the phone, and Marcia could hear her soft cries, and as Marcia hangs up, she agrees.

Only kids.

———

Matt was busy with his homework, she figured, or perhaps nose deep in a video game. Which was good. That gave her more time to get her mind together, brace herself for the impact. She heard the TV shut off and over her, Matt's door closing. He began to walk down the stairs.

Shit, she thought, immediately wishing she wasn't bound to the stupid chair, wished she could just get out of the house. He started to make his way down the stairs, turned into the living room. She heard him as he hopped onto the couch. He clicked on the TV.

"Matt, come here," she managed.

No answer.

She spun around in the wheelchair and grabbed her glass. Went to the counter and rinsed it before filling it from the tap. "Honey, we need to talk-"

That was when she heard the newscast.

"...for more, we go to Channel 5's William Hodges, live on the scene. Bill?"

The camera cut to a static location shot of the high school's sign, and then to a late-thirties reporter with an ugly tie, uglier face red with windburn, and muddled hair. Though you couldn't blame him. The winter wind had picked up that afternoon, the wind chill dropping to the low teens. He stood in front of the gymnasium exterior.

"Ma," Matt called. "Ma, the schools on the news!" He sounded curious, and even, as she knew he would regret, a little excited.

"A sad day for the community here at Reed's Pond Memorial High School, where tragedy has unexpectedly taken the life of a promising young athlete." The camera the cut to the hockey rink, and the reporter continued in voiceover. "It started as a normal day of hockey practice and ended with horseplay which then turned tragic when suddenly, a young student suffered a grave accident." Suddenly there was a quick montage of on-scene police cars, blues flashing while officers milled about, a fancy film-school shot of the rink, starting at the board and zoom-focusing in on the ice, but then -

It was a school picture, the headshot kind with the bad blue background where you pay thirty bucks and six to eight weeks later a package of eight-by-elevens and wallet-size photos show up to your door, but it wasn't any school picture. It was -

"We're being told that the boy, Billy Shaw, lost his footing, and must have slid into the boards. He suffered traumatic injuries."

Matt looked up.

"Ma!" He shouted. "Ma, something- what the hell- Ma."

"Sadly," the reporter continued, paramedics were unable to save the boy, who…"

Matt didn't hear anymore. The world turned to white noise and thunder and ringing and screaming and silence. And in the kitchen, slumped in her wheelchair Marcia Rode keeps thinking *Only Kids*.

Only Kids.

Only Kids.

Chapter Fifteen

The line outside Montgomery Funeral Home stretched a quarter mile down the street. Quite a feat, considering the four inches of fresh snow and thirty mile-per-hour winds. School was suspended for the occasion, it being a Tuesday, and there were camera crews from all of the local stations, and even one network affiliate. Dozens of kids that Matt would swear couldn't place Billy out of a lineup stood in turn; whether they were actually there to pay their respects or to maybe try to get on camera, he couldn't tell. In truth, neither would surprise him. *These fake fucking kids*, he thought, and felt his stomach barrel over and tighten. Through no desire of his own, Billy Shaw had become a celebrity.

Matt had pulled up with his father, Donald, behind the wheel of their blue Volvo sedan. Donald Rode was a quiet man, most of the time. Matt could count on one hand the times he ever truly had lashed out at him, but even then, it wasn't with a shout or a yell. He held his disciplined fist with a sternness only bested by ex-Marines, which he was. No, Donald was a lot of things; a drinker, a monogamous husband, and a business analyst for one of the largest firms on State Street. But what he wasn't, was loud.

He let the car idle, the radio playing soft rock.

"I never told you this, Matt," he began. "When I was a kid, a little older than you, actually, I lost a friend." Matt didn't turn to him.

"Back where I grew up, in Ipswich. Tommy Ryan. We were out at Crane's Beach. You know that one? Right near the orchards?"

"Yeah," he whispered, almost able to smell the honeycrisp apples and cider donuts. "Dad, not now. I don't think I can handle this right now. Please?" The song on the radio turned to Toto, and Matt wondered how Steve Lukather couldn't know that a girl like her could make him feel so sad. In his experience with pop-culture, wasn't it always the ones you loved that left you?

"Please, Matt. Let me speak," Donald said in a voice hushed with patience. "It was October. Off season. Right after Hurricane Belle hit in July. There were lobster traps and buoys all over the sand. We weren't supposed to be at the beach, but we'd had a beautiful Indian summer, so it was warm." His eyes had gone distant. Matt looks out at the line of kids, searching for his friends. "We had gone swimming all morning, Tommy and me - some other guys. The plan, see, was to swim, break for lunch at Farnham's, maybe raise some hell. Who knew, right? Sneak into the estate up on Castle Hill, sneak a quart of Cutty on the dunes in the afternoon."

The line out of the funeral home looked like a snake, twisting gnarled down the sidewalk.

"So, the group of us, we hopped into Joe Smith's dinghy, six of us in a boat that could safely hold three and headed towards Essex over the channel. We were laughing and telling jokes. It was a great time."

Matt's ear fueled between the intimate story his father was telling, and the *Meet you all the way - buh-ba-ba- Rosanna-ah!* of mid-eighties prog.

"We were coming between the marsh and Hog Island." His fingers started tapping the drum beat on the dashboard. "The water was choppy, the currents, sheesh." He took a sip of his small regular from Dunkins, placed the cardboard cup back in the holder. "You never met him, so you wouldn't know. But Tommy was a joker, right? Like how kids are, just a wise-ass. So, he stands up in this tiny boat, and starts doing his best Kennedy bit, talking about Cuba and

Marilyn and DiMaggio. 'That kid could put a smile on a turd,' my mother used to say about him. We lost it, right? Hootin' and hollerin' like he was a hot shit."

Matthew hadn't noticed at first, but his father's speech seemed to choke up a little. "Dad?" he managed.

"The water was really choppy that day, rough. That's when he slipped." He slapped his thigh with a loud clap. "Went over. Just like that."

A tear rolled down his cheek.

"We panicked, right? 'What do we do, What do we do, Oh my god!' But nah." He shook his head. "The undertow was just too strong. He didn't have a chance. He was there one minute and gone."

Matt unbuckled the seatbelt. He had never heard his father talk so openly before. He was almost terrified by the honesty.

"The local police come out, Coast Guard. They drag the water for three days. *Three* days! Know what they found? Nothing. Ever. No body for his mother to cry over, nothing. He had an open casket wake with a framed picture in his Yankee's shirt. And that was one he would have never lived down. Can you believe it? The last time anyone's gonna see ya, and you wear the wrong team."

He chuckled a little, swallowing the sound. "But you know, it gets better, Matt. Not all at once and I can't say it will happen anytime soon. But it does. Hell, your mother and I got married out on that island."

"I thought you were from Providence?"

"Ah, no, your mother, we met at Salve Regina. But got married on the Hog. And we took you up to the orchards a few times, and they're just down the road. But that's the thing, Matt. You can't let the bad in your life define you, who you are." He took a long, slow breath. Exhaled. "This is going to be okay, Matt. Not now, but it will."

He'd have never taken his father, the same man he saw put on a shirt and tie and take the commuter rail into Boston five days a week, as ever having much insight into the world. The things you never knew about your parents could blow your mind.

"You sure you're ready for this?" Don asked his son.

"No," said Matt through a hoarse and breathy voice, and made to get up. Stopped. "Just," he started. He sat back down. It felt like the rate of gravity became exponentially stronger the harder he tried to leave the car. "Dad?" he asked.

"Yes?"

"Why'd he have to? Why'd he have to die?"

And then the tears were coming, streaming down his face. It hurt. It burned. He hadn't remembered crying this hard in god knows how long. After awhile, they stopped.

"Does it ever stop?" Matthew asked. "The hurt?"

His father held him close.

"I don't know."

Matthew sat in his room, wondering where Conway was. It'd been six hours. Right? He had his daily meeting with Dr. Tso at 1:30, which was exciting for a change. Matt actually got upset, shouting at the doctor when he suggested that maybe Matt was the kind of person that didn't need to get more sleep. Even with the trazadone he was only averaging four hours a night at most. And when he stormed out of the exam room at half past two, slamming the door behind him with an echo that screamed down the halls, poor Mrs. Jackson toppled over her Jenga blocks.

"Sorry. I'm sorry," he said. He decided a shower would be good.

After, he looked in the bathroom mirror and cringed. His body looked gaunt. Had he really lost so much weight? He'd lost his appetite a few days ago, after Allie stopped visiting, but he didn't expect such dramatic results. She had stopped calling. And when he finally had the urge to try her phone, a nasally message came up stating "The number you have reached -insert pause-is not in service." So that was it, he thought. Just a few weeks apart and she's changing her number. Doesn't call, doesn't visit. What good was it with him in here and her out there?

The mirror. His face, the lines. He seemed to have aged five years in ten minutes.

Cat didn't know what to do. Standing outside the school band-hall, she was pacing back and forth, deciding on whether to use that payphone. So many thoughts. He had *seen* her. She was a witness to a murder. The television newsman had said it was an accident, what happened to Billy. And everyone believed it! That's what was the worst part. The principal had made a solemn declaration during morning announcements the day following the murder. She hadn't slept in a week because she knew, just knew that PJ could be lurking in the shadows, creeping, staring with that cold, dead grin.

She was also terrified about what she was about to do. But she saw her hand picking up the receiver, dialing the ten-digits for the police station. After two rings, a voice said, "Police. How may I direct your call?"

"Detective Johnson, please."

"Please hold," the voice said. The line went blank, and for a split second she thought it had disconnected, but then she heard the transfer sound and felt both relief and angst.

"Where's Conway?"

It was right after the last group of the night, and Matt sat in the TV room with four other patients and Trisha, the night orderly. The group meeting had been "Conquering Procrastination: How We Choose To Delay Getting Healthy." It was a crock of shit, Matt had told them. He was cranky. He missed his friend.

"Who?" Trisha had replied. The orderlies worked on staggered shifts and, this being the Short-Term Unit, had a high turnover rate, so it wasn't exactly odd for one person to not know the names of all thirty people under their watch at any given time.

"Conway! Zach Conway. He's an older guy, mustache. Crew cut. Speaks in poetry."

"Yes," Trisha said. "Well, sometimes patients aren't able to come to group. And sometimes they are discharged-"

"Discharged? What?" he shouted and banged his hand on the coffee table, which caused a quiet mousy girl in a hooded sweatshirt to curl up on the couch and squeak. "He didn't even say 'Bye.' How can you let someone go without saying bye to their friends?"

"Matthew," she started. "I don't know any patient by that name. I checked my list, just now. There's no one here named Zach Conway."

"That's bullshit!" he said, starting to pant. "He's my friend and you let him leave? Where...where does he- I mean, when will he be back? Is he ever coming back?"

He began pacing back and forth between the television and the window, the chicken wire glass taunting him. He began to cackle like a maniacal witch. An unknown urge came to him then and he started beating his chest with closed fists. His hands raised until they were punching his head. All at once he kicked the coffee table sending activity sheets and colored pencils flying across the room like missles. Suddenly, without warning, Matt found himself on the ground. As he struggled, Matt saw for an instance that the face of the thing that had collided with him was a fifteen-year-old boy.

It was PJ Armstrong. He was smiling.

Matthew didn't flinch.

"Help," he heard the nurse call, as PJ squeezed his arms around Matt in a bearhug. "Somebody get somebody! Quick. Somebody call a doctor. He's gone-ooooofff!"

PJ found himself on his side. Matthew had kicked him off, climbed on top and began pummeling his face. The patients screamed and ran from the room with a hurried one-two, one-two. Trisha, still trying to remain calm in the chaos, didn't know whether to approach, or to run screaming for help.

"You. Fucking. Bastard!" Matt accentuated each word with a punch to the boy's face. The boy was a mess, broken nose, swollen eye. He could barely gasp for breath let alone scream. Matt screeched with hysterical laughter, an almost euphoria covered in blood. "You. Fuck-." And suddenly he froze, time slowed, his vision became blurry. PJ's face disappeared, and, in its place was the broken face of a young man, a man Matt knew. Garrett, a tubby 24-year-old janitor who worked part-time on weekends to pay through a culinary arts degree at Newbury, who had been mopping just outside the door of the group room, who must have seen the commotion and, trying to relive his glory days playing starting defense for Waltham High, tackled Matthew with a crash, pinning his shoulders to the floor, which, though carpeted, hurt like a motherfucker. Just a kid who got paid eleven bucks an hour.

Garrett. Not PJ Armstrong.

Matthew stopped, collapsed on the floor.

―――

He came to, couldn't tell if it was an hour later or a week. He was in a room he'd never seen before. It was similar to his own room, but there was no window. One bed anchored to the floor by bolts. He tried to sit up but felt a pressure; tried to raise his arms-

"What is this?" he began. "Re... Restraints? Are you kidding me?" he said.

Dr. Tso sat in a chair. "Mmhmm."

"What did you give me?"

"Benzodiazepine," he said. "500 mg through the arm. Not the longest lasting effect but works like a charm in these kinds of...situations."

"Situations? Doc. Listen, I-"

"No, it's time for you to listen, Mr. Rode. We've tried time and time again, but it doesn't seem to be working. None of this. You sure did a number on Mr. Stroud! Put him in the infirmary."

"Who?" Matthew said.

"Not sure if that's the short-term anterograde amnesia, or if you honestly don't know the man who mops your floors everyday. Garrett. He's Garrett. And now we have to deal with workers compensation claims and lawyers. He's liable to sue, for all we know!" He leaned over, opened his briefcase and pulled out a file that looked as thick as the Yellow Pages. He thumbed it open to a random spot in the middle. Began -

"'July 6th, 1997 - Matthew Rode, age fifteen. Admitted for acute psychotic break while in the care of the Mountainview Home for Boys in Gardner, Massachusetts. Patient attacked fellow patient, 17-year-old Casabian Koltov, after fight in the cafeteria. Rode stabbed boy with a fork in the neck after taunting his limp. Koltov survived but has lingering partial facial paralysis.'" He looked up from the papers, into Matt's eyes. "Here's another. 'September 22nd, 1999 - Matthew Rode, age seventeen, admitted to igniting fire that hospitalized 12-year-old Victoria Wilson of North Reading, Massachusetts while camping at Harold Parker State Forest. She was treated for second degree burns to thirty percent of her body, including feet and groin.'"

"That was a camping accident. I forgot to smother the ashes. They flared up. She was chasing a kite and tripped into the pit. It wasn't intentional."

He looked at Dr. Tso. "What? You're gonna read me my records? Don't think you can tell me something about me that I don't already -"

"No, Mr. Rode. You are going to work with me. If you ever want to heal, ever want to try to get well, you need to work with me. I'm calling the shots, now. We've tried medication, hypnotherapy, ECT. All of them - you've either-"

"Wait, wait, wait. ECT? Like, shock treatments?" Matt barked. "I never consented to-"

"It's not as barbaric as it seems, not like *Requiem For A Dream* or anything, but that's besides the point. You consented to treatment by being here, Mr. Rode. I can pull up the boilerplate you signed, if you'd like, but really? It'd be a waste."

He took a long hard look at Matthew, wiped his brow.

"As I was saying. No matter what we try, you've just gone about your business in a stupor, or you've reacted like you did with Mr. Stroud. You have a type of unhinged brutality when triggered, it seems."

"No, no I haven't! I've never attacked anyone. Ever."

"Matthew," Dr. Tso began, "One of the side effects of ECT is *memory loss*." He paused like he really wanted to let that sink in. "Memory loss. Get me? And I can't keep doing these same treatments over and over with no results, Matt. You're a fascinating case and-"

"Fuck you!"

"-and I really think we'd have a chance for success. But I need you to trust me. I need you to open up. Above all, I need you to *want to heal*."

Matt wanted to scream. To dig his eyes out. But he didn't really.

"Here's the one that gets me, Matt. 'April 12th, 1996. Matthew Rode - age fourteen - admitted to Mountain View Home for Boys in Gardner, Massachusetts after plea arrangement on second-degree manslaughter charges. You were fourteen, Matt."

"I don't want to speak about that."

"You were fourteen, dammit. What the hell happened?"

"I want to talk to my wife," Matt said. "Please."

Tso took a sip of what Matt could only assume was water. "And you will, Matthew, you will. But for right now, we need to have this talk. If I'm going to learn anything from you, the first thing I need is to hear it from you."

Matthew closed his eyes.

"I don't want to talk about that. Not now. Not now."

Dr. Tso sighed. He stood and walked towards the door. Knock, knock. The door opened, two orderlies standing at either side of the doorway. "We're done here, Matthew. Until you decide how this goes," he said. "We're finished."

"Like that?" Matt asked.

Dr. Tso waved his arm out the door. *After you*. When Matt doesn't stand, the doctor begins to exit.

Matt tilted his head to the side and tried to stop his leg from bouncing.

"Wait. Doc, wait!" He kept walking and Matt said, "If I tell you, can you guarantee I can see my family?"

This caused the doctor to stop. He turned to Matt. "You want guarantees, Sears is at Chestnut Hill." His feet took off down the hall, which was good, because Matt felt like if he had the chance, he'd paint the damn hall with his blood.

He leapt to his feet and made it to the door and was screaming, screaming after the doctor. "You're just going to leave me? Like that?"

But the doctor was already gone.

———

For three days Matt stayed in the Quiet Room. It was for his own safety, Dr. Tso told him. And each morning he gave him the same spiel about wanting to heal, and each morning Matt told him to fuck off a canyon. They were beginning to sound like real buddies.

Probably the only good part about the Quiet Room was that it gave him time to think things through. He wasn't restrained anymore, which was good. And he could sleep whenever the hell he pleased. Also good.

But he kept thinking back on what that nurse said. Trisha. About Conway. "No one by that name." Horseshit. Unless he gave a pseudonym. I mean, he did say that some famous people were treated from time to time, professors, intellectuals. Who's to say that Matt would have recognized a Rhodes Scholar as easily as Kevin Bacon, right? The only logical explanation in all of this, that's what it was. What it had to be. Because if it wasn't that-

No.

Fuck that right the hell off.

———

Dr. Tso's office was much like the man himself- small, neat, and not quite on the level, Matt thought. He pulled up a chair - the doctor didn't have a couch in order to maintain eye contact- and said, "If I do this. If I tell you everything, what then? Do I get to leave? See my family? What?"

"Matthew," he began. "Healing is a process. It works slowly. It takes time. Think the tortoise."

"But what do I get if-"

"Peace of mind, for starters. How's that?" he asked. "Let's start there and see where we end up. Fair?"

Matt put his head in his hand, rubbed his temples and squinted.

"Okay, doc, Matthew said. "Ok."

Part Four:

Blood On The Tracks

Chapter Sixteen

The day that everything changed, Cat Dawson was searching in the field behind Mrs. Jackson's home for bluebells and Quaker ladies, lilies and irises. Cat was alone, save for her headphones and camera. Normally, on a day like today, she would have wanted to be with Nicki. She had a green thumb and knew all sorts about flowers. But there had been a terrible fight after Billy's death, and Cat had blamed her friend. She opened her locker one Tuesday morning to find the word *SLUT* in large, ugly lipstick written on the back of her locker. When she became openly upset, weeping and searching for comfort from her friend, Nicki was more than cold.

"Well, isn't that true?" she asked. "I mean, Danny and Corey said that you really had a time with them down at the bridge."

"What" Cat erupted through tears. "Why would you, or anyone for that matter, believe something that either of those assholes said. You know me!" She was hurt. "I was assaulted, you, you bitch!"

She didn't know that someone you had known since kindergarten, that had taught you to French-braid, that you confided your inner-most secrets too could hurt you so much.

So, Nicki was out.

And she had spent less and less time with the boys that Spring. Ever since she was attacked at the bridge - although Matt saved her - she didn't know how to trust the opposite sex again. Her dad. Detective Johnson. Not quite a third-waver, she didn't even know what feminism was. And she knew it wasn't Matt's fault; she loved him and knew he was a good person. A decent person. But there was something else about him, like the way he attacked that boy. He nearly broke his leg. It was an electricity she didn't quite know if she liked. Not yet. She was still too young to understand why Pretty

In Pink sucked, that you don't try to tame the wild boys; you just get your heart broken when everyone knows you should have gone home with Ducky in the end. Even if he did save her, she didn't want to be caught up in anything so...she sighed. Life with the boys, she had discovered, was one of ruthlessness and bloodshed. They were still friends, always would be. But she felt, for now at least, it was in her best interest to keep her distance. He excited her and terrified her and for this she felt ashamed. And then there was the fact that she was the only one who saw what PJ did to Billy. But she couldn't think of that. She still spent nights sleepless, hearing the terrible thud his body made collapsing into the boards, the squeak of his skate scraping the ice.

So, she was searching for wildflowers.

Like Matt had told her the previous year, her eighth grade English class had just finished their unit on the transcendentalists, and Mrs. Dauphinee, a staunch and wordy Republican in her late fifties who always wore floral scarves no matter the season, had assigned her class a project based mostly on *Walden*. It was a huge project. The project lasted all semester, focusing on the Alcotts and Hawthornes and Ralph Waldo Emerson. And now that they had finished Thoreau, it made more sense. They were tasked to create a photo album of their own private refuge complete with an essay on the importance of self-reliance and how they could adapt the philosophy to their own modern lives. Cat had purchased many a disposable Kodak from the CVS downtown, and had already filled fourteen pages worth with snapshots of the various fauna around her neighborhood. That camera also came in handy to document felonies, she thought, but she couldn't - not now.

She knew there were great crops of bluestars and irises that grew along the embankment near the thicket that she would love to add to the collection. She also knew the likelihood of finding any now was slim, since there were still dirty snow packs in some parts of town. It would be another two weeks before the lake fully thawed.

BOYS, BROKEN

Her book bag was sprawled along a blackberry bush hanging from a mass of brambles. She wore a hooded sweatshirt, unzipped, over her *Around the Fur* tour t-shirt she had begged Chucky to buy for her. Her foam Sony headphones covered her ears, playing the chorus-drenched distortion noise of Rivers Cuomo. It was because of the particularly gnarly feedback from the bridge of *Only In Dreams* that she didn't hear the footsteps coming from behind her.

Matt wasn't going to try out for baseball that spring, his cleats hung on a peg in his closet collecting dust. After the funeral, he was a wreck, they all were a wreck. Vic Shaw stood in the procession shaking hands in a cold grip that was more distant than his glazed over eyes. "His breath," Donald Rode had told him, "You could almost taste the Ripple on it."

But Matt didn't blame him. He may have been an asshole, but he was still an asshole who lost his only kid. And even though it made him want to grab the man by the lapels of his cheap suit and scream *"Who do you think you're kidding, huh? You never loved Billy. You never loved him!"* he didn't. People grieve in different ways, and to lose a son was something Matt knew he would never know.

Three Mondays in a row through March, they got four to five more inches of wet, heavy snow. On one of the occasions, the wind had been so strong it knocked over the poplar tree in front of the cul de sac near the Shelby's house on Lake Drive. A transformer went over on the Westside and there was a near drowning on the reservoir when a homeless man fell through the ice.

But then, like that, it was April. But it wasn't a case of instant warmth and budding flowers. No, it had been a long thaw, and on Tuesday the 23rd, there was still some doubt about whether or not the annual carnival would take place at the middle school. It was one of their annual traditions, The Gang, buying an "all you can ride" bracelet for eight bucks and riding the Zipper, over and over, until Cat screamed to stop, or Billy puked.

Billy, Matt thought.

But it hurt too much to think about. No, it didn't matter if it was eighty degrees and sunny, if the thing was free and came with a blowjob room. He wasn't going this year.

———

Chucky had been at home waiting for Cat to come back. They were going to have lunch, and then meet Matt up at the Shire around 1:30. But here it was, almost 1:00 now, and Cat was nowhere to be see.

He went to the kitchen, picked up the receiver and dialed. Matt answered after the second ring.

"Have you seen Cat?"

"Not today, Chuck," Matt said. "Have you tried Nicki's?"

"No," Chucky said, knowing that Matt knew that Nicki didn't really hang with his sister anymore. They had some falling out last autumn over something stupid, he couldn't remember what, to be honest. But when it came to teenage girls, could they even keep it all on track? "I don't think she'd be with her. What should we do?"

Matt thought.

"Well, I could come by and we could wait, then go up the fort. Or, we could leave a note for her -"

"I'll meet you up there," Chucky said. It was an easy decision.

———

PJ knew exactly what he was doing, or so he thought. He had been following that bitch since the day he saw her tits, spray painted all Dayglo. He knew she was there at his practice, watching. When he threw that freshman into the boards, he knew she'd liked it. Had to. He remembered her there, taking all those pictures at the rink. Mementos. What girl didn't like to have pictures of a big strong guy tucked away in her underwear drawer? *Unless she was a lezzie*, he thought. *She'd give it to me. Have to.* Unless she's already done so with that gimp or someone else. But he doubted it. She would be all his.

He could see that she didn't see him coming, her face looking back at a notebook in the damn bushes. "Hey, babe," he said.

She didn't flinch.

"Hey, sweety," he said, this time louder, but again, nothing. Then he heard it - it sounded like a bass guitar. *"Da da da da-dee, duh duh duh da-dee..."*

Weezer, he thought. Pretty cool taste in music.

The girl, still oblivious to what or who was behind her, kept cataloging in her notebook. But then she saw the shadow of something creeping up and turned. She didn't scream when she saw PJ but would have if her voice hadn't been stuck in her throat. Instead, her eyes went wide, her freckles seemed to pop off her face with a flush. Immediately she felt as if her stomach would empty. Her kidneys hurt. Adrenaline for all the wrong reasons. There was no where to go. No one to go to. This monster had her where no one knew she was, and she felt her eyes itch as the ragweed and dust blew in the tall grass.

"Hiya, toots," PJ said.

And then he was on her.

Chapter Seventeen

The ascent up to the fort was particularly gruesome. The steep incline, which was difficult in the autumn with the moss-covered rocks, became damn near impossible with the melting ice and mud. By the time Matt reached the Shire, he was out of breath, his hands collapsed onto his knees as he tried to catch his breath.

He called out for his friend.

No answer.

He tried again. "Chucky! Hey, Chuck!"

This time he heard a coughing sound from inside the fort. He ran to the door, opened it to find his friend sprawled on the ground, his face black and blue. "Shit," he exclaimed, opening the cooler, hands searching for ice.

"None in there. Already tried," Chucky said. He was bleeding from his nose. His glasses were on the ground, one lens spider-webbed in fracture. He held up a piece of paper. Matt took it. It was like something out of a movie. A blank sheet, probably printer paper, with magazine letter cut outs.

All it said was "We have her."

"Danny? Corey?"

But he already knew.

"Those fuckers," Matt finished. The air in the school bus was damp. The comforting smell of nature that he had grown accustomed to was absent. It was only now that it dawned on him that they had been recklessly climbing to an abandoned vehicle when Cat was probably on the other side of town. "Dammit we're so dumb."

Chucky sat up. "How do I look? Honest."

Matt shrugged.

"Like you want to kick some ass."

"Thanks, asshat."

"That's Mister Asshat to you, good sir."

Chucky shook his head. "Matt, they're…"

Ping.

Ping.

Ping.

What the fuck was that, a BB gun? Matt looked out the busted window, the one Cat had laced with fabric curtains, and got an inch-and-a-half stone right under his right eye.

"Shheeee," he moaned, his hands going up to his face. Blood dripped onto his fingertips, the soft tissue already beginning to swell. He stumbled towards the door. Chucky grabbed his leg.

"Don't! They aren't fucking around, Matt."

Chucky looked frightened, and not just frightened. He looked *scared*, in a way your leader isn't supposed to look scared.

"Like I am?" Matt said. "Know the best thing about having a friend like me, Chuck? I'd do anything for you. Take a fucking bullet. Believe me?" But he was charging the door before Chucky could answer.

In front of the bus, the air became stiff. Matt figured he was surrounded since he didn't see anyone, but he also knew that the only place to hide would be behind the few barren trees. The branches wouldn't provide any cover since they had yet to bud. And most were skinnier than the torsos of high school boys.

But he didn't have to search long. Out from behind a blackberry bush came both Danny Johnson and Corey Whitaker. Danny was holding a hockey stick, Corey an aluminum bat.

"So, fuckstick," Corey said. "Looks like you made some enhancements to your baby fort."

"Yeah," Danny added. "Have to say, it's actually pretty cool how you guys did all this. Who thought it up?"

Silence.

"Okee dokee," Danny said. He reached into his pocket and grabbed a handful of something. Tossed it in the air and swung.

Ping.

Something hit Matt in the arm. Again, he swung.

Ping.

Another.

Ping.

Danny was hitting rocks half the size of Bic lighters. So that's what the sound was, how he was able to hit me like a damn bullet. And suddenly, for some reason, he started to laugh.

"What are you laughing at, boy?" Corey said.

"Yeah, Rode," Danny agreed. "I'm gonna fucking kill you, you sonofabitch."

But he kept laughing.

"Fucking, stop it!" Danny shouted.

Matt said, "I always knew you couldn't really pitch for shit, Danny. And now I know you can't hit, either!" And he was off laughing again.

The noise was what bothered Danny Johnson the most. Not his pride, or the memory of being embarrassed in front of the crowd during the postseason, but right now. This fucking laughing Gimp. But then he saw his eyes.

"Corey," Matt said. "You want to do yourself a favor?"

"What's that, Rode," answered the galoot.

"Go fuck ya'self," he said, and charged, but towards Corey. This took both boys by surprise. Corey, who had only been flanking Matt when the skirmish began, had been holding his hockey stick low, unprepared to swing. It was easy to grab onto, and Matt used his shoulder to check him hard, stumbling until he fell into the side of the bus with a BOOSH. By the time Danny had figured out what had happened, Matt already held the Bauer in his hands and was slowly making his way towards Danny.

Danny Johnson turned and dashed behind the blackberry bush, maybe looking for more ammo. Matt couldn't tell. What he did know, though, was that Corey was still behind him. True, he was unarmed, but he was still big, and Matt had only pushed him hard enough to get his weapon. He knew hadn't done any actual damage.

He spun and turned his sights back on Corey, stumbling to his feet. "Hey, Core," Matt said, and swung. Corey tried to block the attack, was hit in the forearm with a slash.

"*Eeya*," he groaned.

This gave Matt just enough time to wind up, and swing across his face like he was swinging for the fences. The stick broke over Corey Whitaker's skull, and he dropped. When Matt was satisfied that he wasn't getting up for now, he turned towards the blackberry bush and-

THUNK!

The blow had come across his back. Danny may have been dumb, but he still had a goddam aluminum bat and wasn't afraid to use it. "Fuck you, you crip!" he shrieked at Matthew Rode, and as he raised the bat over his head, Matt braced for the hit that would no-doubt kill him, end his short, 14-year-old life when suddenly Danny dropped the bat.

Matt was confused. As was Danny, or so it seemed. He took two side-steps back, and fell down hard on his bottom, as if taking a seat that was pulled from underneath. His mouth was agape with silent sobs, as if something hurt so bad that he couldn't actuate words. Behind him stood Chucky, a ball-peen hammer which he had swung like a Louisville into Danny's shoulder blades.

Everybody hurt. But not everyone was there. Chucky jumped on top of Danny while he had the chance, pinned his shoulders with his knees.

"Where is she?" Chucky shouted and punched him in the face.

"Fuck...*you*," he managed in a breathy flow, which, as it turns out, was not the answer Chucky was looking for. He picked up a rock the size of a paperback novel and raised it over his head, shocking himself to see he was crying now. "I will fucking kill you," Chucky said. "Where is my sister?"

Danny spat blood. "You know where she is." And to the shock of Chucky, the boy smirked at him. And as Chucky tried to bring the rock down, as he wanted to, his hand was stopped, the rock falling and rolling away. And when he looked up, he wasn't surprised to see his friend, Matt. He pulled Chucky to his feet.

"Forget it, Chuck. She needs us. Let's go."

Chapter Eighteen

And now, they were running, down the hill at breakneck speeds. Matt almost got his foot caught in an exposed root sticking out of the side, would have gone rolling down the hill if it weren't for Chucky shouting, "Jump!" And he did, missing the root by inches, the weight of gravity pulling him closer down the hill.

They reached Scolaro's back yard, hopped the fence, and Chucky started down Walnut Hill. Matt shouted, "Chucky! This way." and turned, heading down Elm Street towards the Jackson house.

They were silent now, focused on the race, cutting through her yard, smashing through the thicket at the border, and knew by instinct that they were near the train tracks.

The ground was still hard down here, but Matt caught a patch of mud and went sprawling on his face. His cheeks were painted with grime, the front of his sweatshirt sticky with mud clods. Chucky hadn't stopped, was about fifty yards ahead of him by the time he sprawled to his feet. His limp, which he had been trying to ignore, was acting up in spades. Every footfall was sheer agony, bright and sharp and terrible. But he didn't have a fuck to give, no. She needed him.

And when they slid down the muddy incline, Matt's hooded sweatshirt got caught again, this time on the hard clay, pulling it up to his shoulder blades. The rough dirt scraped a layer of skin off his side in a twisted rash.

"Ah!" he winced.

Chucky stopped, turned to his friend. "You okay?"

"Yeah," Matt said. His exposed flesh was raw and bloody. "Out of breath. And my leg. Acting up real bad."

The scream that came next cut through the air like a siren.

Matt and Chucky's eyes met. Matt looked worried, but said, "Go. I'm right behind you."

His feet hit the dirt and he was kicking up mud as he ran. "Come on, Matt. Come on!"

"Right behind you," Matt shouted. And he would be soon enough.

"Doc," Matthew says. "I think I need a break. This is getting a little intense, all these memories. I'm sorry."

The doctor looked up from his notes, but he didn't shut off his tape recorder.

"But, hold on. You knocked out one of the kids, Corey, with a hockey stick, and the other with -"

"That was Chucky," Matt said. "Corey was all me, though."

He checked off something in his notes.

"Doc, can we take a break?" Matt looked exhausted.

"No, no," Dr. Tso said quietly. "That's fine. I understand the terrible anguish you must be going through, reliving this."

"You sure?"

"Of course. How about we meet back this evening, after dinner. Get some rest. Relax. Please, be my guest."

Matt stood.

"Thank you, Doc. Thank you."

"Of course," Dr. Tso said. "And Matthew?" He looked up.

"Doc?"

"You will find your old room is back to normal, set up like you had it. And, if you'd like, you are back to Level 2."

"I can have visitors?" Matt asked.

"You may," the doctor said. "Just remember to come back after dinner. I'll be here."

Matt left the office, heard the door latch behind him, and headed back to his room.

"Matt?"

He was just coming out of a dream, a short nap after the appointment with Dr. Tso. When he looked out to the doorway, he saw a face of someone he hadn't seen in twenty years. He was handsome. Older, just as Matt was, his wire glasses missing. *He must be wearing contacts*, he thought. *Or maybe lasik.* But he knew who it was instantly.

"*Chucky?*" he said. "Fuck, man, how the hell are you? How did you know I was -"

"Don't worry about that, Matty," Chucky said. God, he couldn't remember the last time anyone called him Matty. He felt like a kid again. He stood, walked to his friend, and embraced. It felt good to be in the arms of a friend, and not being held down by an orderly. When he pulled away, he could tell that tears were streaming down his face.

"I'm sorry, man," Matt said. "But, I just can't believe it. I was just talking about you in my session. Fuck. I mean, dammit. This is all too weird." He gave off a slight chuckle. "Wanna go for a walk?"

"Can you do that?"

Matt smiled. "Chuck, when my best friend comes by, I can do what I want. Come on."

Chucky wore a light jacket and blue jeans, his hands in his pockets. August had turned into September and the cool breeze of oncoming autumn was in the air, but Matt didn't wear a sweatshirt. He preferred to feel the breeze on his skin like he was a sponge sopping up nature.

"Here," he told Chucky as he pointed to a bench. The two sat in silence, breathing in the air, spying the leaves on the oaks and maples knowing their day was soon to come.

"Beautiful campus," Chucky said at last.

"It is," Matt replied. "You know what they say. 'If you're gonna get sick, make sure to get sick in Boston.' We got a good place going here, Chuck."

"And your doctors, the staff - they're good, too?"

Matt thought about it for a second.

"Yes. They are. I mean, at first I didn't know what to make of the place. Right? Like, it's very go-at-your-own pace, which I was never good at, you know?"

Chucky nodded.

Matt looked at his friend. "It's like they don't force anything on you. They expect you to take the time to heal, I guess. Which is what made it so hard at first. No one pulling the strings, but, like, *everyone* pulling 'em? Right? Damn, man it's just so good to see you!"

Immediately his thoughts raced back to when he first saw Chucky standing in his doorway.

"Did Allie tell you I was here?"

There was silence from Chucky. He looked away.

"Goddammit," Matt said. "She doesn't talk to me for over a month, won't call, won't visit."

"You sound mad," Chucky said.

Matt reached up into the air, then put his hands on his head. "Not mad, no," he said. "It's just...frustrating. I can't tell what's going on. I don't even know if she's okay. Or, and this is huge, but what if she's having papers drawn up so she can leave me here? Right? Just take Gabe and go off with daddy in the nuthouse?"

"Frustrating, yeah. I can see why you would feel that way," Chucky said. "Everything out here, must seem like it's moving a mile a minute, and you're stuck inside. I get it." Chucky's eyes drifted off into the distance towards the Rec Hall. "What's in there?"

Matt looked at where he was pointing. "Ah, not much. Basketball court. Weight room. Used to have this friend, Zach. We would shoot hoops."

"Zach?"

BOYS, BROKEN

"Yeah, Zach. Conway. He was a professor or a private school teacher or something. Old guy, but a wicked hook-shot."

"That's good, Matt. Real good," Chucky said. "*It's real good to have friends.*" His voice seemed to have shifted on that last part, not sarcasm, but it had a sternness Matt didn't feel comfortable about. He looked and for a moment Chucky was fourteen, his glasses, a single lens spider-webbed and cracked.

"Chuck?"

"It's really good to have friends, Matt," younger Chucky said. "Friends that have your back, that you know would take a fucking bullet for you if need be, right?"

Matt was was terrified. There was a shift, all right. A big freaking shift, and Chucky, who wasn't Chucky, began to speak in a kind of monotone, suddenly seemed to hold all the cards in a game Matt didn't realize they were playing.

"Chuck, you okay. What's your problem, man?"

"My problem, Matt?" And now he was older again, but now he wasn't Chucky, he was a girl, maybe Cat? Or how Cat would look if he knew how she would look? But that wasn't right, either, because now he was Young Chucky, again. "Maybe you go back in there with Dr. Tso and you let him know everything and you'll remember. Maybe then you'll see why I would have the right to be a little upset right now, Matt. Okay?"

"How did you know his name?"

"You know why, Matt. You know why."

None of this was good. Matt wanted to leave. He needed to dose. He needed to sleep. He needed to scream. But he didn't know how to do any of that without dealing with this ghost friend. This smiling, creeping death.

Matt took a breath and began.

"Chucky, okay, what is going on, man. I can't do this. I can't see you like this, man, because, right now there's something...there's something wrong with you, man!" Matt shouted. "I've never lied to you. I haven't seen you in twenty goddamn years and now you're accusing me? Big guy! Fuck you, man. If you can't see, I'm not really in the best place here, right now. Get it? Do you understand?"

"Bull shit. Remember what happened under that fucking bridge, Matt? You said you'd be right behind me. Were you?"

"Yes!"

"But *were* you?" Chucky said, "because last I remember, I don't think I saw you after you fell. And everytime *you* fell, who was there, huh? Me. Every single time. But the one time *I* needed *you*?"

Matt stopped.

"I," he began. "I was, Chucky. I *was*. You know I would never do anything-" but he trailed off. This isn't what he wanted, to fight with an old friend, if that's what he could even call it. Matt bent over to tie his shoe.

"You go back there," Chucky said. "Will you? You tell him? About me, about Cat?"

When he looked up, he had to do a complete three-sixty.

Chucky was gone.

Chapter Nineteen

"I remember, Doc."

Matt hadn't burst into the room insomuch as knocked the damn door down. Dr. Tso was still in the middle of eating his reheated tilapia filets, the smell of microwaved fish heavy in the air.

"Okay," Tso said. "If you give me a sec-"

"No, it has to be now. Right now," Matt said as he paced back and forth, the drawstring in his sweatpants bouncing against his crotch.

"But I need to get my recorder, right?" he asked. "We need to have this on tape, Matthew. Just like before."

A light went off in Matt's head.

"She was taking pictures," he said.

"Apropos of nothing, that was." Dr. Tso hit the red Record button on the machine.

"No, doc. Cat was taking pictures. I remember. All over town that spring. She was doing some English project. I had the same one the year before. And I told her that down in Ms. Jackson's yard, they had the best wildflowers there."

Dr. Tso still looked confused.

"You may continue, Mr. Rode."

"If it weren't for me telling her where to go, none of it would have happened," Matt declared. "Don't you see?"

"But Mr. Rode," Dr. Tso said, shaking his head. "You still haven't told me what *did* occur. What happened under the bridge?"

"But I *am* telling you."

Matt looked right into the doctor's eyes.

"Chucky," he said.

"Chucky?"

Matt nodded.

Matt had doubled-back. He climbed up the embankment, the thick clay providing an easy enough foothold on the way up and stayed inside the bushes closest to the edge of the fall down cliff. Once inside the thicket, it was a slow crawl, but he knew that if he could just get to the bridge without being seen, he could out flank anyone else there. It wasn't the best plan, but given the circumstances, it was the only thing he could come up with.

But then he changed his mind once he saw it. Strewn across the branch of one of the blackberry bushes was what appeared to be a torn black t-shirt. He stared at it and saw the front, right where it had been cut open. *Around The Fur.*

"Jesus," he whispered aloud.

He burst from the bush and was running, screaming down the tracks.

"Chucky! Chucky, he's got her. He's got a knife!" His feet, one-two one-two off of the ties, kicking rocks covered in dirt and snow with his Chuck Taylors. "Got a knife!"

His feet hurt; his leg was in agony. His side was cramped, his breath tasted like metal. "Chucky! Chucky!" But he kept running, and when he turned the bend, when the bridge came into view and he saw the reality of the situation, everything stopped.

PJ was on top of Cat. She looked bad, her face bloody, her top clothes missing. She was only in her underwear which PJ was having a hell of a time trying to remove with all of her flailing. Her camera lay beside her.

"Quit it, lovey," he moaned into her ear. "It'll be so much better if you don't fight."

She screamed. One of his arms was pressed hard against her windpipe, and now she was choking.

"You took some pictures of me," PJ said, reaching for the camera with one outstretched arm, his eyes never losing hers. "I take...some pictures...of you." He strained as he reached.

Matt looked for Chucky, and at first, didn't see anything, until he saw what looked like a pile of red rags further up the hill. It looked like someone had used them to rinse out a bunch of red paint brushes. But as he inched closer, it started to make sense. It was his friend, and he wasn't moving.

"No!" He ran to Chucky, sliding into the dirt like he had hit a double. "No no no no no!" His words came out trampled. Chucky's broken glasses lay next to his body, the one lens a starburst fracture. They would never help anyone to see again. His throat had been opened with the big, ugly knife, and now he had two smiles.

Cat's choking gags broke Matt's concentration. He looked up and saw that PJ had removed her panties. Too fast. Everything happening too fast. And now that step was complete. He would have her if Matt didn't intervene, didn't do something now to save this little girl. Matt saw himself bolting at the giant, kicking and punching and clawing, ready to slay it with whatever power he could muster. But then he saw he was still standing where he had been. His mind was moving ahead of his body, his legs frozen in terrific panic. The screams were terrible. Her eyes finally met his and she didn't need to mouth the words. He felt his legs lift. Help was on its way.

PJ was unaware of the teenager hurtling towards him from behind until he heard the "Grrrrraaaa!" of the shout coming from some monster's guts. He was hit hard with a tackle, flying off of the girl, and when he looked to see what truck had hit him, only saw the Gimp.

PJ grabbed the knife at his feet and before he could look up, was hit in the face with a piece of firewood.

"You killed him!" Matt shrieked, and hit him again, this time the log coming down on his shoulders. "I'm gonna kill you, PJ!" He swung again. "You're dead!"

PJ knelt as if he was proposing, the knife tumbling somewhere out of sight. But PJ shook off the attack like it was no big deal being smashed with a log, and slammed his fist into Matt's face, blood spewing from his mouth and now broken nose. He flew onto his back and tumbled onto the cold gravel, the taste of copper oozing down his throat. Tears streamed down his cheeks. "Eeee…" Matt cried. Lying there, he could see his misty-red breath in the cold air. He could hear a rumbling in the distance from the oncoming train. And then he could feel himself being pulled up from his collar as PJ yanked him with one arm, throwing his free fist across his jaw. The pain was sudden and dull, his whole body on the defense, just ready to call Uncle.

"You're all dead," PJ moaned. "That hockey kid. Chucky. And pretty soon, both of you."

The rumbling grew louder, and PJ got to his feet. Stumbling, he looked for the knife, eyes searching, head whipping back and forth.

"Where," he screamed. "Where the fuck is it?"

PJ made a startled face as if he was just spooked by a ghost, felt a tremendous pressure in the small of his back, and then a warmth is his pants as if he had sat in something sticky. He reached his hand back to where the sensation was coming from, and when he brought it forth, became confused. His hand was covered in blood. He turned to meet eye to eye with the brutalized girl he had almost had. She was holding his knife.

"Mine…" he murmured.

The tracks began to rumble, the train only fifty yards or so away. PJ stumbled. For a moment he forgot how to breathe.

"Here," Cat screamed. "You can have it." And she tossed the knife onto the tracks. And when PJ turned again to look for the blade, the horn of the train blaring a deafening roar, going too fast to stop now, that was when Cat pushed him.

———

Author's note: The following report was first published in the evening edition of the Reedy Pond Ledger, April 23rd, 1998 by City Desk reporter Chuck King -

It was a tragedy on Tuesday afternoon, witnesses report, as the 4:15 Haverhill line, which had just made its stop in Reading Center, struck and killed a Reedy Pond high school student. PJ Armstrong, age 16, was pronounced dead at the scene by paramedics. Some witnesses on the train stated that it looked as if Armstrong leapt in front of the oncoming train, though that hasn't been confirmed. Police say the body of another boy, 14-year-old Charles Dawson, was also found nearby. Authorities have not provided much detail into the cause of death, but have stated that for the time being, they are considering the two deaths related. One other teen, whose name has not yet been released due to his age, we're being told, was also questioned by police. Meanwhile, as the community mourns, everyone in the small hamlet are trying to figure out what could have possibly happened to cause such a loss.

———

Dr. Tso looked up from his notes, pressed Stop on the recorder.
He took a sip of his coffee.
"So, it was both of you?"
Matt let out a long sigh. "But Cat never...I never let her say anything." He was chewing on the tip of his thumb nail. It made a grotesque clicking. "I took the fall for it. For everything."

"But you didn't kill him, Matt. It's not like you pled to stealing a Snickers from the 7-11. This was huge."

Matt shrugged. "I couldn't save Chucky. But I could save her. The cops show up, see one kid with his throat torn out, an underage girl bloody and naked. I tried to save them. That was my defense, why I got the plea deal in the first place."

"And why they sent you off to Mountain View."

Matt didn't move for a long time.

Chapter Twenty

"I think I've given you what you wanted, Doc. How's about your end of the bargain?" The session had ended thirty minutes ago, but Matt insisted on waiting outside the office door to catch Dr. Tso as he left.

"You'd like to see your," he sneezed. "Your family?"

Matt smiled.

"The arrangements may take a little bit of time, but I assure you. I'll take you to see them personally."

"Off campus," Matt asked. That was even better than he imagined.

"Off campus, correct," Dr. Tso said. He opened his office door and waved Matt out. "I'll let you know as soon as everything is in place."

"Should I call her?"

"What?"

"Should I call her," Matt repeated. "You know. Let her know we're coming?" He pushed his hair back and rubbed his eyes.

The doctor shook his head. "That won't be necessary, Matthew," he said, and continued down the hall. Later that night, Matthew lay in bed, across from an empty mattress. His former roommate must have been discharged, but that worked out well. He had the whole place to himself, had the windows, the trees, the moonlight. He listened as the baby blackbirds and jays cried out for their supper. And for the first time in weeks, Matthew slept without dreaming.

It was early, about 6:30 AM, when he heard the knock on his door. It was Garrett, the orderly, followed by Dr. Tso. They were both wearing fleece-lined pullovers in navy blue and orange, the hospital's colors. Garrett tossed Matt a similarly colored sweatshirt, sweatpants, and a pair of Nikes.

"Put these on," Garrett said.

Matt looked up confused. "Why can't I wear my own clothes?"

"Because," Dr. Tso said, "It's a little chilly this morning. And since we're transporting you, you need to wear the...uniform, if you will."

"But Allie," he said. "Won't this, like, embarrass her? If any of her neighbors saw me dressed like - "

"None of your neighbors will see you, I assure you," Tso said.

"Like I told you before, I've made all of the arrangements."

They were loaded onto a small white passenger van with ambulance flashers on top. The flashers weren't on, of course, but it had them just in case, Matt supposed.

They pulled out onto the parkway, and headed for 128 South, which turned into 93 North in a spectacularly fucked up highway planning design that only Massachusetts could come up with. For the most part, they drove in silence. When they took the exit for South Boston, Matt suddenly felt an urge of unease.

"Matthew," Dr. Tso said suddenly. "Do you remember why you were admitted into my care?"

Matt looked confused in the rearview. *What do you mean by that*, he thought. "What do you mean?" he said. "Of course, I do. Suicidal. Weird thoughts. Stress. Was gonna end up on the sidewalk outside Boylston."

"Mmhmm."

BOYS, BROKEN

The van drove past Broadway station, turned and headed down Dorchester. They reached the rotary, and turned towards Day Boulevard, headed towards Castle Island and Pleasure Bay. A fort on Castle Island, now a peninsula, was erected in 1634 by the British to protect Boston's shipping interests. It was changed to Fort Independence after the Revolution, and during World War II, was used by the Navy as a degaussing station. The Point, once a neighborhood of proud Lithuanian and Irish blue-collars, firefighters and mechanics and shop owners, was slowly becoming a neighborhood of condos and sky-high rents only the rich transplants could afford. And now Castle Island was run as a state park. There was a hotdog stand covered in joggers and mothers pushing strollers, new-development families moving into a gentrified City Point with no idea of its lore save for Hollywood. The old power plant loomed over the point, the old timers that once worked third shift would have been disgusted to see the traffic on Broadway caused by coffee shops and sushi bars, hair salons and pet-friendly thrift stores.

The van pulled into the parking lot and idled.

"Doc," Matthew finally said. "What are we doing here?" He hadn't been this close to home in a long time. It was amazing to think that any second, he could run into Allie with Gabe on her shoulders, strolling down to get a hot dog or slush out at Sully's.

Dr. Tso took off his seatbelt, opened the door and hopped out. Matthew unbuckled and followed suit. They walked to a bench near the canoe rental shack and sat. After a moment, Dr. Tso pulled out a pack of Winstons. He took one out, lit it. Offered the pack to Matt.

"Thank you," Matt said, inhaling deeply. They were silent for a long while as they enjoyed their cigarettes, blue smoke curling around fingertips stained with nicotine.

"Where's Allie?" He looked around. "They gonna meet us?"

"Shortly," Tso nodded. "I've been thinking about our session from yesterday. You remembered that fight so vividly, Matt. It was surreal. I have to say it must have taken a great toll on you." He took a drag off his cigarette. "That said, I'm still not sure we're there yet."

"What d'ya mean?" Matt asked.

"I don't think you got everything right. For example, you mentioned that PJ tried to rape Catherine? That she was naked, flailing about, but still had the wherewithal to stab him? Would you be surprised to know that when I scoured the newspapers, the microfiche, the only person they found alive at that bridge was a boy? You, Matt. That they never mentioned finding a girl at all?"

"I don't know what else to say. My mind. It jumbles sometimes. Maybe I forgot that she took off into the bushes," Matt said. He was shaking now. "Tried to hide. She was naked and afraid, right?"

"Maybe," said Tso. "But maybe she wasn't there that day. Was she attacked by that boy, probably? Possibly even assaulted like you said. But what if it happened in September instead of April, or even the year before? How do you even know you were there to save her? How do you know, Matt, that you didn't just kill that boy in a fit of rage? That he got in a fight with your friend, Chucky, and you attacked him. Or worse, what if you and Chucky were both targeting him - what if you were the bullies?"

He stopped. Pulled out another cigarette. "Of course, we don't know any of that. Don't think I'm implying that as fact. I'm not, and it isn't. Not really. And we couldn't ask her, Matt, because Catherine Dawson of Reedy Pond was killed in a fender bender with a Crown Victoria while in college in the Berkshires. She was rear-ended, the shock triggered her asthma, couldn't reach her inhaler in time. She died on the scene."

"Cat's dead?"

"No, she's not, Matt," the doctor said. "I just made that up. See how easy it is to lie? Now, I'm not suggesting you made that story up. I'm just trying to help you understand how easy it is to forget the details. How easy your mind can play tricks? Remember when I told you we'd tried everything on you?" He lit the butt, pulled, blew trails through his nose. From his profile it reminded Matt of a dragon. "Hypnosis, ECT, controlled substances, clozapine, risperidone?"

"Yes," Matt answered in a numb haze. The sun peeked through the gray clouds in spots, trying to fight its way through. It gave Matt a headache.

"And do you have any idea how long it would take to competently measure any lasting effect any of those treatments may have on you? Do you have any idea how long you've been under my care? Can you remember? Try. Think really hard, Matt."

Matt sat in silence. A group of teenage girls passed by on mountain bikes, the tires thump-thump-thumping on the boardwalk as they headed towards the hotdog stand. "Well, I tried to jump August 3rd, was admitted the next day. And knowing Halloween is in a few weeks, I'd say just under two solid months." He leaned and put his hands through his hair, massaged the back of his neck. It was now a killer migraine.

Dr. Tso nodded again. He ashed into an empty soda can that lay next to the bench, offered it to Matt.

"These things will kill you, right?" Matt grabbed the can and threw it onto the beach. "Doc, where's my family?"

"When you first came to me, it wasn't two months ago. Understand, yes, you had been suicidal, had tried to jump off that building. But that admission was in June of 2012. You were here for two weeks and then released. You were assigned a counselor, you had your list of medications, your wife had a treatment plan. You went home to your child. Everything seemed to be going on track and you continued with your treatment until-"

"Until what?"

"Until the accident," Tso finished.

"Accident?" Matt asked. Tso continued.

"The accident, Mr. Rode, occurred during a particularly warm indian summer that year. I remember it so clearly because it was on the news, and I saw your face, so grief stricken and sad, and I felt for you because I had remembered you. Your first admission, well, you made quite the impression. Remember how you'd play the piano? You led most groups. Hell, you were the posterboy example of a person who had nowhere to turn to, but through the grace of god understood he needed help. That was you." He put his hand on Matt's shoulder, squeezed. "You, your wife, Allie, and Gabriel were on a boat in the Choate Island channel near Essex."

"No, we weren't. You're getting you notes mixed up, Doc. That was my father's story. And it's Hogg Island," Matt said.

"Yes, yes you were. A man in a speedboat had gone by you a little too fast, the wake capsized the dinghy. Gabriel hadn't been wearing his life jacket. He goes under. Almost at once, your wife dove in after him but…"

Immediately Matthew is there. The smell of the marsh, the taste of the salt in the air, the rainbow puddle of excess gasoline in the water. The quiet purr of the outboard motor. Gabe was wearing boat-shoes, Sperrys. They looked comically small on his toddler feet. He was so excited. Allie had on a trendy throwback sixties one-piece. He wore board shorts and a striped polo. But, no, that couldn't have possibly happened.

"But the undertow, right?" Matt agreed.

Tso nodded, inhaled the last of his cigarette. He stubbed it out and flicked it like you would a coin. "Because that was my dad's story, doc. I told you that before. He was a teenager and his friends were out partying and-"

"Your father died in the car accident," he said. "When you were a kid."

"No," Matt said. He was very confused now. Then, "No! That was this other guy. Sandy. Sandy! He was helping my mother. He was driving me to the hospital."

"Your *mother* was driving you to the hospital, Matt. And she was drunk. Your father reached over to grab the wheel. That's why you crashed into that truck."

None of this made any sense.

"No, no," he said. "None of that is right. You are wrong."

"Your father never made it, Matt. Died at the scene. Your mother, yes, she was hurt. But she never became paralyzed, Matt. Doesn't get to visit you as often as you want. But it doesn't get easier." Matt's cigarette was now burned to the filter, the cherry coal scarring between his knuckles like the worst game show prize in history. He dropped it.

"Do you have any idea what year it is? Matt, it's 2017. You've been under my care at Knott's for five years. *Five.*" He emphasized the last word, hanging on it like a wet sock on the line. "That's longer than your son was alive. Longer than you were married."

"Fucking stop talking about my family like they were just some cast of characters in a play. Just stop it!"

Tso continued.

"The man in the boat, Mr. Conway, had been drinking. He was arrested but you dropped the charges. You were mourning and just wanted to grieve. Or so I thought." He smacked his hands together with a BOOM. Matt's eyes shook in his skull. "Two months later, you end up back here, under my watch. When they sectioned you at the hospital that night, you had been screaming the name 'Zach Conway.' In your car, besides a picture of your wife and son, the police found a man hogtied in the trunk. He wasn't hurt but had been screaming something about a 'Rambo knife.' This is all in your file. Care to see?"

Matt flipped him the bird.

"I looked up the news report on the accident. That guy that caused it, his name? Zach Conway."

"That's bullshit. This is all fucking bullshit!" Matt screamed. Tears were streaming down his face.

"Attempted murder and kidnapping, Mr. Rode. The only reason you got sent to me instead of upstate with the real characters was because of your sob story to the jury. You weren't in your right frame of mind, which everyone agreed on. And given our history, I was assigned to figure you out. To figure this out. And I need to know everything I can to make sense of this. Because I thought I had fixed you. I thought you'd be better. We were making some serious strides, here. Then you started having the hallucinations, talking about Zach Conway and how great a friend he was. Playing basketball with ghosts of people you couldn't possibly have known. Phantoms, Mr. Rode. You attacked Garrett." He sighed. "We tried everything, Matthew. Everything. But then it dawned on us that this wasn't a simple case of mania, you weren't depressed; you have acute schizophrenia, Matthew. It's the only way this works."

"Fuck this," Matt said. "Fuck you. I don't believe a single word of this. None of what you're saying could possibly be true. Schizophrenics aren't even violent!"

"But you are, Matt. You are violent. Even as a kid. This is simply the truth. It is. Your family-"

"They aren't dead, doctor, and I'm not crazy. Don't try to sell me on that. They aren't dead. How would you know, huh?" he asked. "I would know. Want to know why? Because you don't know how it felt to lay beside her, you arm curled around her waist, feeling her belly rise and fall with each slow breath, knowing that inside was a life. A life I had made."

"Matt," he said.

"No, you wouldn't know what it's like going to doctor's appointments, having him get tubes cause of his chronic ear infections, might have to get a bone-anchored hearing aid. You don't get to tell me what I know about my family, doc. If they are alive, or-" he paused. "Or not, it's just not that simple. And it certainly isn't up to you."

Matthew stood and walked to the van. The seat was cold, and the stench of the cigarettes hung on his sweatshirt. Outside the windows, the sky had faded to a dull gray over the Atlantic, the wind caused the gulls over the Sugar Bowl to look as if suspended in time. On the bench, Dr. Tso sat and finished his smoke as the joggers and cyclists moved around in a damn hurry.

Chapter Twenty-One

As the van approaches the parking lot, Matt sees the giant wrought iron gates surrounding the entrance like spears aimed at the clouds. Protecting us from ourselves, he thinks, his mind in a daze. He hasn't spoken for the thirty-five minutes of traffic they had been sitting in on Storrow Drive. In fact, it occurred to him that no one seemed to speak much at all. When they come to a stop, the van nestling close to a large, brown group of Boxwood topiary, he realizes that they are not at the hospital.

Pinewood Cemetery sat upon 130-acres of hills and ponds and farmland grass clipped as neat as a putting green, three miles north of South Boston. It was built in July of 1865, just after the Civil War had come to an end, as a place for the dead Union boys to lay at rest; their statues and gravestones were often marked with inscriptions of poppies, signifying peace and slumber and rest. The rows of tombstones and crypts and mausoleums were accented by dots of flowering azalea, rose, and Japanese Holly bushes, as well as giant oak and cedar trees.

Much like the city itself, the cemetery's design didn't prove useful to navigating a car; the paths and roads bisected each other at odd angles, winding in and out of roads and trails once used by horses and cows. Along these paths were a few trash cans littered with the dead stems and petals of rotting flowers, the remnants of memories collected in fibrous colors. Near these, benches ran along the roads and trails. A place to rest in the restful place.

"No," Matt said when the van stopped. "Just forget it. I'm not, I'm just not getting out."

Dr. Tso unbuckled and waited, sitting in the passenger seat. Outside, a mist had developed. Rain would be soon. With the engine off, the air inside the van turned humid, the windows starting to fog up.

"Didn't you hear me? I said forget it, doc," Matt continued, his voice a tired, swollen mess. "Have that orderly drive us back. I can stay here all day." He scratched at the whiskers on his chin; beards always started out itchy. The doctor didn't say anything. Instead, he flipped through his clipboard, mindlessly humming the theme to *Jeopardy*.

"Cut it out," Matt said. But the humming only got louder. After a few seconds, Garrett joined in.

"Seriously!" Matt said. "My head is killing me." And he wasn't wrong. His migraine had permeated into his shoulders and the base of his neck. He raced his hand over his shoulder and started massaging the flesh, kneading and kneading and kneading; anything to relieve the tension.

Outside of the van, raindrops started to dot and dash across the windshield, the pavement, the grass. The mist disappeared and now it was full rain, the spatter and plip-plop ricocheting off the hood of the van in popcorn bursts. Every instance was a firecracker of bright pain in Matt's head.

"Row thirteen, four stones in from the sidewalk," Dr. Tso said. He enjoyed cemeteries as much as he enjoyed eating sand. "We'll wait here."

He sat for a few more moments before he realized they were serious. "Doc, I..." he gulped. "I don't know if I-" And he looked at the doctor with such a sad longing. "...Alone?"

"Alone, Matthew. You have to."

BOYS, BROKEN

The air was thick with rain, the water dripping off his hood in wet gobs. As he made his trek through the stones along the path, past rows four and five and six, the water pooling into puddles off the edge of the grass, he began talking aloud. "Stay calm, Matt, just stay calm. You can do this, Matt. Matt." And he passed rows eight and nine and ten, turned to make sure the van was still there - it was, that was good - and continued. "This is like, just an exercise, right? Just like shooting hoops. No big deal. Just going to see your family's plot, right? Completely normal afternoon behavior, right?"

There was a crash of thunder that sounded too close for Matt's comfort, and now the rain was sheets. His parka didn't matter anymore. He'd be just as good shirtless. He made it to row twelve when his sneaker went wild under his foot, slipping in the mud and sending him sprawling onto his face. He'd done that before. He pushed himself to his feet, the front of his body caked with dirt and grass. He was soaked. When he wiped the rain out of his eyes, when his vision finally came back to him, that was when he saw it. Could it be real? Just four feet in front of him.

The tombstone wasn't a stone at all, but a rectangular marker in the ground, half covered in wispy grass. A single rose lay dying in the rain. The inscription was simple. It read:

Gabriel Arthur Rode
B. Feb 4, 2007 - D. Aug 3, 2012
"May angels lead you in. Hear you me, my friend."

Leaves rustled in the trees as the wind picked up in gales. The pain. It didn't hurt, no. It *tore* and it *cooked* and it *burst* from inside until Matt found himself on his knees, clothes utterly destroyed with nature, wanting to sob, to scream and heave and wrench himself into the sky like the lunatic fringe. Yes, he wanted to scream, and he wanted to plead, and to moan. *If there was a God, any God at all*, Matt thought, *he better show himself right now, dammit, because Matthew Rode was fucking calling him out! Better yet, strike him dead with a bolt of lightning so he could meet face-to-face and he could show what a few dozen years of lapsed-Catholicism could do.*

But he didn't. Instead, he was still bawling and weeping into the ether when he heard a sound from behind. "I'm sorry, Matthew. I really am. But I had to-"

"No!" Matt screamed, collecting himself and standing in the rain like a slug. He sneered at the doctor with a look that said *Don't You Dare*. "You didn't have to do shit! I get it, okay? Alright? 'Matt's had a breakthrough,' right? He knows he's a looney-tune.'"

"Matt, please."

"No, doc. I get it. I get it. I get it!" And he spat on the ground, the saliva and phlegm running rivulets into a storm drain. "So, where is she?" Matt asked after catching his breath.

"Who?"

"The fuck you mean, 'Who,' Doc? My wife! Where's her damn stone!" Matt said. "Or did we bury Allie on the other side, and I have to go walking on my hands like an acrobat through the mud to find her in Row Four-Fifty-Six-Double-Z?"

"Matt," the doctor said. "Please, listen."

"No, *you* listen!" Matt jabbed a pointed finger at Tso. "You listen to me. I can't do this anymore, doc. You should have never let me outside cause I'm feeling like running onto the Pike right now and playing chicken with the semis. I can't. I believe you, but no more, okay?"

"Dammit, Matt, your wife's not dead."

He stomped towards the doctor, his breathing louder.

"You said...but you said that my family-"

"No, Matt, *you* said your family was dead."

Did I, Matt thought. At this point he couldn't make heads or tails. "Like I told you before, your mind plays tricks. Think, dammit." Matt's face was frightened. Confused. Angry. "Think! Yes, poor Gabriel drowned in that ocean, but your wife, Matt? Come on! Remember."

BOYS, BROKEN

And as the rain drips out of his soaked shirt, again he is lifted out of the rain, out of the gray sky and the cemetary cold, and back onto a summer dinghy on Cape Ann being splashed by salt water, during what should have been a peaceful afternoon of chowder and steamers, but turned into the be-all and end-all of trainwrecks. And he sees her go down in after their son, not once, but *three* times, deeper and deeper with each pass, her breath being held longer and longer. And he sees himself, diving in after her, pulling and grasping until he catches her writhing hair, and wrenches her from the undertow, *sans puer*. Yes, he remembers, yes, as he arched her back along the marsh, giving her chest compressions until her swollen lungs coughed out salt-water in choking, ugly bursts. He remembers the silhouette of her body against a police van off of Conomo Point, the evening dark casting shadows on both mother and father draped in blankets and drinking black coffee from a thermos as the dive team made their third pass. He can see the sad, lonely eyes that adorn her face later that autumn, and how cold it felt when she stared through his. The first Christmas without gifts, the empty pull-out couch; this he all remembers. And he remembers that spring, when something finally snapped and Matt decided that whoever did this to his son, whoever destroyed his family, whoever made his wife a cold hard fragment of herself well, he didn't deserve much of anything, right? Certainly not to live a happy life. And he remembers the knife, and the phonecalls to Conway's house. How it was almost too easy, catching him in his driveway making hook-shots into a too-short net. He remembers.

"But...where? How?" Matt asked, his eyes red and swollen, but not a single tear can come. His face is utterly spent. "I, I call. I call her all the time. And nobody...nobody answers. Ever. Nobody."

"I can't say, Matt. Honestly, I don't know why." And the rain began to taper off, slowly, until the big wet sheets were just drops hanging in the wind. He put his hand on Matt's shoulder. "But she's still around. I don't know where she lives. What she's up to. But she's around."

"How can you know that, Doc?" Matt said.

And Tso says, "Who do you think left that rose there?"

Matt looked back at the dead flower on the marker, and then stared at the van, it's door beckoning to be opened.

"I shut her out?"

"Must have," the doctor said, nodding. They start to walk back towards the van, Matt's laces sloshing in the puddles. Through the spotted windshield he saw the bruised and bandaged face of Garrett and felt sick.

"Does she...does she visit?" Matt asked, and Tso shook his head.

"But you can't judge whether or not someone loves you with how often she visits. It's just not that simple, Matt. Doesn't work that way."

―――

They return to Knott's Haven, pass through the ancient, brooding gates and stop. Garrett gets out first, unlocks Matt's door. He unbuckles and hops out of the van. Dr. Tso had been silent for most of the trip back to campus. In fact, besides the zoo crew on the classic rock station, the only sounds he could remember hearing were the specks of gravel on the highway and the occasional scream of a Lindsey Buckingham guitar solo.

"Alright, Matt. Come on." Garrett leads him by the shoulder and as they enter the main Admissions Building, as he always does, he stares up at the birds flying overhead and wonders if they know they're free.

―――

He walks ahead of the doctor and they both veer off in different directions, Tso to his office, and Matt to the group room. He grabs the remote, the old CRT popping on, the picture fading in from dusty glass. He surfs through the channels, stops on the news, but almost reconsiders. What's the point of catching up in a world that's full of war and greed and poverty? Where families are torn apart. Where kids die at hockey games, or school shootings, or terminal illness. Why add to the grief when you spend your days staring at the gray stucco walls in here?

No, he switched off the tube.

Later at dinner as he ate his mashed potatoes, he looked up from his corner seat and noticed new faces in the cafeteria, a white girl of about twenty, her black hair cascading past her shoulders; a black man in his thirties, tall and fit. He smiled at Matt and he nodded in reply. And though you never, ever ask, he wanted to nudge the man and say, "Borderline personality," or "schizophrenia?" Just to see what the reaction would be. The new crop. Babes in the woods. Though to be honest, he had no idea if they had been here three hours or three weeks. He hadn't been paying much attention lately. His mind got jumbled from time to time.

Epilogue

He lay in bed, eyes open, shut, open, praying for sleep to come. But his hand kept tapping his left leg right above the scar. He looked out of his window and the clouds separated, giving view to an orchestra of starlight, and he saw his hand reach up and grasp the beam that shone through the window, pull himself up and through the chicken wire mesh and suddenly he was out! Outside at night, his bare feet on the cool grass, the autumn night caressing his skin.

And for a moment he could see himself as a boy, only this wasn't the crippled boy, victim of a car accident; it was a boy who could run without stopping, who could skate on the ice, climb mountains, and play football without worry. It was a boy who could swim without feeling the cold titanium rod that held his upper leg to his pelvic bone. And it was summer, and his friends were there, all of them. The twins, Nicki, Billy, Chucky, and Cat. They held the world in their grasp, would never know the tragedy of having potential and never living up to it. Matt wanted to do everything, start fires, play chicken, anything at all to feel alive. He could fly or run or jump his way to freedom-

He was in his bed.

He considered getting up, going to the john. But he didn't. Instead, he reached into the desk drawer and pulled out his shredded copy of *The Alchemist*. He thumbed through to a passage he had highlighted some time ago. He began mumbling over and over. "We lose control of what's happening…world's greatest lie…"

He read the passage over and over again, and again, and for a few more hours, supine on his plastic mattress, the clock in the hallway tick-tick-ticking away the night. And as his eyes grew heavy from exhaustion, his mind and body aching from the days events, as the book collapses on his chest, as the orderlies come and lift him by the armpits, place him on the gurney, wheel him to the Big Building, as the IV is administered and the electrodes are placed bilaterally on his temples, Matthew Rode sleeps.

So, where were we, Matt thinks. Building up armies on Australia, trying for a land grab of Asia. But that wasn't right. Cat was building up for Chucky. Billy had North America in between slapshots. Armies upon armies, growing. The thing about *Risk* he didn't like so much is that Matt had started with a shitty hand, and it kept getting harder and harder to play for everyone else when you knew you were going to lose in the end. Sometimes, occasionally, he wanted to be selfish, to have everybody else battle it out while he sat back planning how to strike. But he never did.

No, they had always been running. From the Sox. From the Johnsons and Whitakers and Armstrongs of the world. From adults who were absent or abusive or dead. From themselves.

They ran to flee danger and to prevent tragedy. They ran early and they ran late, and the monsters were always on their heels. They were broken kids; porcelain dolls trying to collect all the shards and glue them back together. It wasn't their fault that some pieces were never found or were set in the wrong place.

JONATHAN MITCHELL

The truth, he decided, was that they ran because they were kids, once, and they would always be running. It's just what kids do. It had been springtime, he remembers, and they were running. Running for their lives.

ABOUT THE AUTHOR

Jonathan Mitchell is a husband, father, and writer. In his spare time, he enjoys cooking, playing guitar and recording music. He lives in Boston with his wife and son. You can follow him on Twitter @jmitchellwrites.

Made in the USA
Coppell, TX
16 February 2024